GROWING UP — UP — KATIE

A PRETEEN NOVEL

STEVE F. HALLSEY

ISBN 979-8-89309-436-7 (Paperback)
ISBN 979-8-89309-437-4 (Digital)

Covenant Books
11661 Hwy 707
Murrells Inlet, SC 29576
www.covenantbooks.com

To my granddaughter, Camden.
She brightens every room she enters. She is the bravest
girl I know.
She will always be my Pierce.

CHAPTER 1

"I'm scared," sighed Mikey as he watched the movers carry the last pieces of furniture out of the house and pack them snuggly into the moving van. Tears rolled down his soft, round cheeks and fell on the old gray wood porch floor where he stood. He was seven years old and felt like his entire world was falling apart and being packed away piece by piece into the truck.

"I'm scared too," replied his sister Katie, "but I know everything will be okay." She grabbed his hand and held it tight, and together, they watched as one of the movers closed the big door to the moving van and locked it with a large padlock.

Katie was eight years older than Mikey, and as his big sister, she knew she had to be brave and make him feel better about their move to the big city of Chicago, but she was as frightened as he was. She felt like crying too.

"But I don't want to leave our house and friends." He sobbed.

"I know," said Katie, "but we need to look at this as an adventure and a chance to meet new friends."

"I don't want new friends."

"Mikey, I know this move is hard on you, but Mom needs to be in Chicago for her new job, and we need to support her by being happy and positive."

"I'm not happy or positive."

"You will when we get there," she lied. "You'll see. You'll soon forget all your friends here because you'll have so many new ones."

They sat cross-legged on the porch and watched as the big moving truck pulled away from the curb and started its long journey from Alpine, Utah, to Chicago, Illinois. Katie wrapped strands of her long blond hair around her finger and pulled at it absentmindedly.

She knew if their father were still alive, they wouldn't have to move, that her mother wouldn't have to take a job in Chicago, and they could stay in the house—the house she and Mikey had been born in, the only house they had ever known.

Mikey sat there with his chin cupped in his hands and his skinny elbows on his knees. "I'm going to hate Chicago, I just know it," he mumbled, tears still running down his cheeks. "I won't have any friends to play with."

"We're going to have to learn to like Chicago, Mikey," said Katie, "because that's where we're going to live. It's the place where Mom found a job." She reached out and playfully messed Mikey's hair with her fingers.

"Why couldn't she find a job here in Alpine?" he said, swatting her hand away from his head.

"Because Alpine's a little town that doesn't need another dentist. It already has Dr. Williams. Besides, Mom will work with many patients for a big dental practice in Chicago." Katie stood and brushed the dust from her blue denim shorts. "Chicago is a beautiful city with tall buildings, parks, and a river that runs right down the middle. And Lake Michigan takes up one whole side of the city. I've seen pictures of Chicago in my schoolbooks—it looks wonderful."

"If you like it so much, why don't you and Mom go and leave me here? I can take care of myself."

"Don't be silly. You know Mom won't let you stay here alone."

"I can stay with Grandma."

"Grandma's too old to take care of you," said Katie, even though she had had the same thought and asked her mom if she could stay with Grandma. Her mother had said the same thing: that grandma was too old to take care of kids.

The screen door slammed, and Katie's mother walked out. She was a tall, thin woman with dark-brown hair like Mikey's. Her hair was pulled back on her head and tied in a ponytail. She wore an old flannel shirt, blue jeans, and a pair of worn sneakers. Katie recognized the shirt as one of her dad's.

Her mother's face was the shade of a ripe peach, and her eyes were the color of a warm summer sky. To Katie, she looked like an angel, and by coincidence, her name was Angelina Sparrow, but most people called her Dr. Sparrow.

"What are you guys talking about out here?" asked her mother.

"Nothing much," answered Katie. "We were talking about Chicago and how much we're looking forward to the move."

"I don't want to move," said Mikey. "I want to stay here with my friends and Grandma."

"I know you do, champ," said Mom. "And I wish we could, but since your father passed away, I have to support the family, and that means I have to go where there's enough work to feed us."

"But, Mom," cried Mikey.

Katie looked sourly at her little brother as if to say, "Be quiet, and don't make Mom feel any worse than she already does." She had decided to keep a smile on her face even though deep down inside, she wanted to cry and scream, but she knew this would only upset her mother. She knew her mother was trying to do what was best for the family.

"Look, guys," said Mom, "as soon as I finish cleaning the house and lock it up, I'll take you to your favorite smorgasbord restaurant, and you can have all the garbanzo beans you can eat. Is it a deal? After eating, we can rest in the hotel room before our flight to Chicago tomorrow morning."

"Sure, Mom," said Katie. "While you're finishing up, can I run to Camden's house and tell her goodbye?"

"Yes, but be quick. Grandma and I are almost done here. And as for you, Mikey, I want you to stay in the yard where I can see you."

"But, Mom," whined Mikey.

"You heard me, champ."

Katie brushed the rest of the dust off her blouse and pants and walked up the street to Camden's house. Camden was her best friend and had been since first grade. She knew it was going to be extremely hard to tell her goodbye.

She walked up the street, kicking the loose pebbles with the toe of her black running shoes. She knew this would be the last time she would see Camden for a long time—maybe forever. She felt a knot tighten in the pit of her stomach as if she had swallowed a big rock.

She had not left Alpine yet, but already, she felt lonely and scared. Tears began to well up in her eyes, and for the first time since her father died, she began to cry.

She reached the corner and turned left on Oak Street. She could see Camden's red brick house with the big oak tree in front. Seeing the house made her cry even harder as she remembered the many times they had played Barbie dolls under the leafy branches and the snowy days they had spent building snowmen and Eskimo igloos. She remembered laying back on the grass and looking up into the branches as they talked about the boys they liked and the girls in their class they would never be friends with, even if they were the last girls alive.

She reached the pathway that led to Camden's house and wiped her eyes. She didn't want her to see her crying. She wiped her nose on the sleeve of her blouse and walked to the front door. She rang the doorbell and waited.

"Who is it?" called Camden's mother.

"It's me, Katie, Mrs. Stevens. Is Camden home?"

The door opened, and there stood Camden's mother. She had deep red hair that she wore short and spiky and held in place with mousse and hairspray. Her eyes were green with specks of brown around the edges. Katie thought Camden's mom was the coolest mother in the neighborhood.

"Hello, Katie, how are you? Are you ready for your big move to the city?"

"I guess so," said Katie.

"We're going to miss you around here."

"Thank you, Mrs. Stevens, I'm going to miss you too."

"Come in. I'll get Camden. She's in the kitchen doing dishes." Mrs. Stevens turned around and disappeared down the hallway. Katie stood in the entryway and sniffed the air. She could smell the sweet aroma of freshly baked chocolate chip cookies. The smell made her mouth water. The knot in her stomach she had a few minutes ago was replaced with a rumble, and she realized she hadn't eaten since breakfast almost eight hours ago.

"Katie," screamed Camden as she came down the hallway. "I was hoping you'd come by before you left. I have a present for you." Camden grabbed Katie's hand and pulled her down the hallway toward her bedroom.

When they reached the room, they tumbled onto the bed, flipped over on their stomachs, and put the big pink pillow under their chins. Camden reached under the bed and pulled out a package. It was wrapped in bright yellow wrapping paper and tied with a white ribbon and bow. On top of the package was an envelope with Katie's name printed neatly on the front.

"I didn't get you anything," whispered Katie.

"You didn't have to. Your friendship is enough for me."

Katie felt the blood rush to her face as she blushed. She had forgotten to buy Camden a going-away present because she had been packing. She felt terrible that she hadn't got her best friend a gift.

"Open it," said Camden.

Katie sat on the bed and placed the package on her lap. Carefully, she pulled at the scotch tape that held the yellow wrapping paper in place; she didn't want to tear it. Underneath the paper was a pearl-colored box with gold writing on top. The inscription read Devey's Fine Jewelry. She pulled off the cover, and there in a bed of cotton was a beautiful, braided silver bracelet. It sparkled in the warm afternoon light that flooded the room. She lifted the fragile bracelet off the fluffy white cotton and held it to the light. The sunlight danced off its silver surface in flickers and bursts of yellow, gold, and red. On the inside of the bracelet were words etched in a delicate script. The words said, "Friends Forever."

Katie looked at Camden and smiled. She reached out, wrapped her arms around her neck, and hugged her, not a weak sisterly hug, but a best friend hug that said, "I'll never forget you as long as I live."

"Do you like it?" asked Camden.

"Do I like it? I love it."

"That's good because I've been saving all my allowance since Christmas to get you that bracelet.

"It's beautiful," said Katie. She slipped it on her wrist and tightened the clasp to keep it from falling off. "I can't wait to show my mom."

"Will you write me a letter when you get to Chicago?"

"I'll do better than that. I'll write you every day."

"Promise?" asked Camden.

"I promise," said Katie, "and best friends don't lie to each other."

"I'm going to miss you. My mom might let me visit you in Chicago next summer."

"I'd like that."

"Open the card," said Camden. "I picked it out just for you."

Katie slid her fingernail under the envelope's seal and peeled it open. She took out the card. On the front was a picture of a big fluffy cat, and on top, it said, "To My Best Friend." She opened the card and read the words Camden had written; they said, "You may move far away, but you'll always be in my heart. Love, Camden."

"My mom helped me write it," said Camden.

The two friends lay back on the bed, arm in arm, with their heads touching each other, and watched as the sky turned a fiery red as the sun began to set behind the Wasatch. Katie knew this would be the last time she would see Camden and Alpine for a long time.

✄

CHAPTER 2

Katie woke to the sharp metallic ring of the alarm clock. She reached over to the nightstand and turned it off. It took a minute before her head cleared, and she could remember where she was. She looked around the room and realized she was in the hotel room her mother had rented for them the night before. She looked at the other bed and saw Mikey and her mother cuddled together. She missed being young like Mikey and snuggling with her mother in bed. She was too old to do it now.

She got out of bed and tiptoed over to her mother. She bent over and kissed her on the cheek. She knew they had plenty of time to get to the airport. There was no need to wake them now. She let them sleep while she went to the bathroom, showered, and brushed her teeth.

When she finished in the bathroom, she opened the door and saw her mother sitting on the side of the bed, rubbing her back. She looked tired from packing boxes and cleaning the house. "What time is it?" asked her mother.

"It's eight o'clock," said Katie.

"We need to hurry. Grandma will be here at nine o'clock to take us to the airport. Please be quiet while you dress. I want Mikey to sleep until I'm out of the shower. I don't want him whining when we're on the plane."

"Okay, Mom."

Katie dressed, sat at the dressing table near the closet, and brushed her hair. She heard the shower turn off and overheard her mother singing softly as she dried herself. It made Katie happy to hear her mother singing again. She hadn't heard her sing since her father passed away.

7

The bathroom door opened and out rushed a gray-white cloud of steam. Her mother entered the room and yelled, "Where's Mikey!"

Katie jumped from the dressing table and joined her mother. She looked at the empty bed where Mikey had been sleeping.

"Katie, I asked you to watch Mikey," said her mother. "Where is he?"

Katie felt panic fill her body like static electricity. Where had Mikey gone? She hadn't heard him leave or the door open.

"He might be under the bed or hiding in the closet," said Katie. She got down on her knees and looked under both beds—no Mikey. She raced to the closet and threw open the doors—no Mikey.

"Katie, how could you let him out of your sight? How could you let your little brother wander off in a big hotel like this? You're his big sister. You're supposed to look after him."

"I was."

"If you were, you didn't do a very good job of it," said her mother as she pulled on her clothes. "I'll go find him."

"Mom, let me go. I'm already dressed," said Katie.

"You've done enough this morning, don't you think? When will you learn to be more responsible? You're almost sixteen years old. It's time you grew up." Katie's mom buttoned her blouse and wrapped a towel around her wet hair. "You stay here, Katie, and don't move a muscle. Do you understand? I will deal with you after I find Mikey."

Katie slumped down on her bed and watched as her mother rushed from the room. She put her hands over her eyes to keep the tears from running down her cheeks. She knew she had let her mother down. Her mother was already nervous about the move to Chicago, and she had added another level of stress to her already sky-high anxiety. But it hadn't been her fault. Mikey had a mind of his own, and when he wanted to do something, he did it no matter what she said or did to stop him. She felt hurt. She was mad at Mikey for leaving the room and upsetting their mother, but most of all, she was mad at herself for not meeting her mother's expectations.

Ever since her father's death, everyone treated her differently, especially her mother. She talked to her differently and expected her to do more around the house. It was as if her mother now saw her as an adult with adult responsibilities—it was like she was expected to grow up overnight. Her mother expected her to watch Mikey and ensure he did what he was supposed to do. She was expected to help with the shopping and prepare meals.

Grandma also wanted her to do more to help her mother. Katie didn't mind helping, but she wondered when she would have time to grow into these new responsibilities and be allowed to spend time with friends. Since her father's death, she had less and less time to be with her friends and be herself.

She wished her father were still alive. He had been her best friend—someone she could talk to when she had a problem or hug her when she felt low. He was the one who read to her at night and told her stories he made up just for her. If he were here, they wouldn't have to move, and she wouldn't have to grow up so fast and be responsible for Mikey's bad behavior. Why did her father have to die? A new batch of tears welled up in her eyes.

She looked at the bracelet Camden had given her as it dangled on her wrist. She knew she had at least one friend in the world, and now she would leave her to move to Chicago. The thought of leaving her friend was more than she could bear. The thought of losing her dad and Camden made her feel sick to her stomach.

She heard the key slip into the door lock and watched as the door swung open. In walked her mother, pulling Mikey behind her. He was crying as he tried to pull free from his mother's grip. "I don't want to go to Chicago. I want to stay here with my friends," he cried.

"Mikey, I don't have time for this right now," said Katie's mother. "Get dressed. Grandma will be here in a few minutes to take us to the airport, and we can't be late. They won't hold the plane for us."

"I'm not going," said Mikey.

"Do what Mom says," said Katie as she stood from the bed and grabbed Mikey.

"You're not the boss of me," he said.

"She is your boss right now," said his mother. She turned to Katie and added, "Help him dress while I blow-dry my hair. And this time, don't let him escape."

The words stung Katie like the sting from an angry wasp. She hadn't let Mikey escape, yet her mother blamed her for his misdeeds. It wasn't her fault he was a reckless and careless boy.

Katie took Mikey by the arm and led him to the closet while their mother disappeared into the bathroom.

"You're hurting my arm," said Mikey.

"I'm going to do more than hurt your arm," she scolded. She tore at his pajama top and pulled it over his head.

"Mom, Katie's hurting me."

"She can't hear you," said Katie, "the blow-dryer is too loud. Now slip this shirt on and quit being such a little monster." Katie tried to slide the shirt over his head, but he wiggled his head back and forth so she couldn't get it over his curly hair. When she almost had it on, he pushed hard against the bed. Her leg hit the corner of the bed frame, and a sharp pain shot up her spine. She grabbed him again and pulled him toward her. He reached out and slapped her face. She sat there in shock. He had never hit her before.

"Mom, Katie's hurting me," he yelled. Katie heard her mother turn off the hair dryer and stomp into the room.

"Katie, what are you doing?" asked her mother in desperation. "Can't you do the simple job of getting your brother dressed without hurting him? Can't you do anything right? Mikey, come here, and I'll dress you."

Katie, embarrassed and hurt, went to the closet and retrieved her suitcase. She packed her clothes as her mother finished getting Mikey dressed. She fought back the salty tears that blurred her vision. She folded her yellow blouse and placed it in the case. She watched a tear slide off her cheek and splash onto the blouse.

There was a knock on the door. It was Grandma. "Are you guys ready to go to the airport?"

"Not yet," said Katie's mother. "We've had an episode this morning, and we're running behind. Please put Mikey's shoes on while I finish my hair and pack my bag?"

Katie's mother disappeared into the bathroom and shut the door. Grandma looked at Katie and saw her red, puffy eyes. "What's wrong with you?"

"Nothing," said Katie. "I'm sad to be leaving you and my friends."

"Come on, you can tell me."

"Mom blames me for everything. I can't do anything right. Nothing I do pleases her."

"That's not true."

"Yes, it is. I don't think Mom loves me anymore."

"Sure, she does," said Grandma. "Your mother is under a lot of pressure right now. Your father passed away, she's starting a new job, and she's moving you and Mikey to a new city. That is a lot of stress for anyone." Her grandmother finished tying Mikey's shoes and sat him on the bed to watch television.

Grandma walked over to Katie and hugged her. "You know I love you, don't you?"

"Yes, Grandma."

"I need you to be strong and brave right now. I need you to help your mom with this move."

"I know. I wish Dad were still alive. He could fix things."

"I wish he were alive too, but no amount of wishing will bring him back. You, Mikey, and your mom must move on with your lives now. You will have to stick together and make the best of the situation. It's extremely hard on your mother, and we all need to help her make a new start."

Katie nodded her head in agreement and kissed her grandma on the cheek. "You're right, Grandma. I'll try to help the very best I can."

"I know you will."

Katie's mother came out of the bathroom. "It's time to go. Let's start this new adventure."

⤝✄⤜

CHAPTER 3

The movers hadn't arrived yet, and Katie and Mikey sat and looked out the window of their empty, new condo. It was located on the fifty-fourth floor of a new high-rise building, and their view looked over Lake Michigan, Navy Pier, and Lake Shore Drive. The condo was so high in the air that they could see parts of Indiana and Michigan across the lake.

Katie couldn't believe how flat everything looked. There wasn't a mountain in sight. The flatland made her homesick for Alpine and the towering mountains surrounding the little town. She loved hiking in the mountains with her dad during the summer and skiing with him in the winter. They had spent a lot of time in the mountains together, and now there wasn't a mountain anywhere, just flat ground and super tall buildings.

Katie looked over at Mikey, who was playing on the carpet with a small metal car he had brought with him on the plane. "Do you want to play a game, Mikey?" she asked.

"No," he said. "I'm playing cars."

"Then let's draw pictures. I brought an art pad with me in my suitcase."

"No, I want to play cars."

Katie's mother stepped out of the kitchen where she had used her cell phone to call the movers to see where they were and why they hadn't delivered the furniture yet. "Katie, why don't you go downstairs to the lobby? When I was down there a few minutes ago talking to the concierge, I saw two girls that looked to be your age."

"But I don't know them."

"Of course, you don't know them. You just moved here, but if you introduce yourself, you will get to know them. I'm sure they are very nice and would enjoy having a new friend. I can stay here and watch Mikey until the movers arrive. Go ahead, but don't leave the building."

"Okay," said Katie reluctantly. She didn't want to go but was happy to leave the condo for a few minutes and get away from babysitting Mikey.

She grabbed the key that she kept on a silver necklace and put it around her neck. She kissed her mom on the cheek and went to catch the elevator. She had to wait a few minutes for the elevator to arrive on the fifty-fourth floor and then several minutes for the elevator to descend to the ground floor.

When the elevator doors opened, Katie walked down the long hallway from the elevator bank, past the mailbox area, and into the lobby. Sitting on a couch near the front desk where the concierge worked were two girls talking and looking at a fashion magazine, the kind of magazine she had seen in her mother's dentist's office. One girl was short and stocky and wore her curly short hair like the fur on a poodle dog. The other girl was tall and thin and had long brown hair that she wore straight to her shoulders.

Katie stopped. She didn't know what to do next. She didn't know what to say. She wondered if they would like her. She stood there and stared at the girls. The short, stocky girl finally looked up from the magazine and stared back. She put down the magazine and said, "What are you staring at?"

"Nothing," said Katie.

"Then go away and leave us alone. We're busy," she said.

"I thought I might join you," said Katie. "I just moved into the building."

"We don't need anyone else to join us. We're fine the way we are," said the stocky girl. "We're fine all by ourselves."

"Now, Sarah, that's not nice," said the thin girl. "We can always make room for another friend."

"Why?" asked Sarah.

"Because it's polite." The tall, thin girl stood and walked toward Katie. "My name is Tennison, and this very impolite person is Sarah," she continued. She pointed a finger in the direction of the stocky girl. Sarah didn't look at Katie. She turned her head and picked up another magazine. "Don't mind her. It's hard for her to make new friends. Do you like to look at *Vogue*?"

"Yes," said Katie, "but all my magazines are on my iPad and still on the moving truck. My mom, brother, and I are moving in, and the movers haven't arrived yet."

"Where are you moving from?" asked Tennison.

"From Alpine, Utah."

"Utah? Where's that?"

"Out west," said Katie, "about a thousand miles from here."

"Are you a farm girl?" chimed in Sarah.

"No, I'm not from a farm. My mother is a dentist, and my father was a medical doctor."

"Alpine, Utah, certainly sounds like farm country to me," continued Sarah. "Did you wear overalls and a straw hat and say 'shucks' and 'darn'? Do you even know how to read, farmgirl?"

"Don't pay any attention to her," said Tennison. "Normally, she's nice. It takes her a little time to warm up to people she doesn't know."

"She sounds awful mean," whispered Katie.

"You'll get used to her."

"I hope."

"I have an extra magazine. Would you like to join us?" asked Tennison.

"Yes, I sure would," said Katie. The two girls went to the couch and sat.

Tennison reached inside her backpack, pulled out a *Vanity Fair* magazine, and handed it to Katie. "Here, you look at this one, and then we can switch."

"Thank you," replied Katie. She put the magazine in her lap and watched as Tennison pointed out clothes she liked in the *Vogue* magazine she held.

"What are you looking at?" asked Katie.

"We're looking at this year's latest fashions. Our school is having a big back-to-school dance at Navy Pier in a month, and we want to pick out the right outfits," said Tennison. "We want to look our best for all the cute guys there. There are a lot of hot boys at school, and they will be at the dance."

"It's too bad these magazines don't have farm clothes. You could buy a new pair of overalls for the occasion," said Sarah with a snicker. "I'm sure that would make you feel right at home."

"Sarah, be nice," said Tennison. "Katie's new here. Let's make her feel welcome."

"But look how she's dressed," countered Sarah. "She looks like she's from Iowa, where she used to slop the pigs each morning."

Katie looked down at her old blue jeans, faded yellow blouse, and dirty white running shoes. She suddenly felt out of place and embarrassed. Blood rushed to her cheeks and made her face feel hot. Since her father had died, her mother hadn't had time to take her shopping to buy new clothes. She fought back hot tears. "The rest of my clothes are on the moving van," she said.

"Sarah, you can be so nasty and mean," said Tennison. "Katie, you look fine. Don't worry about Sarah. You will learn to like her, just as I have. Let's look for new clothes."

Katie knew she was going to like Tennison a lot. She had come to her rescue and saved her from more teasing from Sarah. She gently touched the bracelet Camden had given her and wondered if Tennison would be her new best friend. She needed a friend right now, someone to talk to, someone she could trust and share secrets with.

The girls talked and looked at the magazines, but Katie could sense Sarah's coldness toward her. Sarah refused to talk to her and only talked to Tennison. She felt invisible.

Although short and stocky, Sarah was a pretty girl with milky white skin and steel blue eyes. Katie detected she was one of the more popular girls her age and that if she couldn't be friends with her, it would make her an outcast and outsider when they went to school in a month. But how would she make Sarah her friend, or at least make her not hate her as much as she does right now?

"Hey, Sarah. Hey, Tennison," a boy's voice sang out. Through the revolving door that led from the street to the lobby of the condo building came one of the most handsome boys Katie had ever seen.

He was tall for his age, and his face looked like a movie star's. His hair was the color of the sand on one of the beaches she had played on when her family had gone to Florida on summer vacation a few years ago. And his eyes were as brown as hazel nuts. Her heart began to race.

"What are you guys up to?" he asked.

Sarah jumped off the couch and ran over to the boy. "Hey, Ryan," she cooed. "We're looking for new school clothes. Where have you been?"

"I was over at the beach by Navy Pier. Who's your new friend?" he asked.

Katie felt his eyes on her face. She wanted to hide behind the couch because of her old clothes and dirty running shoes. She bowed her head and looked helplessly at her lap as Ryan and Sarah walked toward her and Tennison.

"Oh, that's some new girl. Her name is Casie, Kathy, or Karen, something like that," said Sarah as she took Ryan's arm. "She's from Idaho, Nevada, or Arizona. It's one of those states out west that nobody wants to go to. She's a farm girl."

Katie wished there was a hole in the floor she could crawl into and cover herself with dirt. When she looked up, Ryan was standing right in front of her. She thought she was going to die at once. He was so handsome.

"Hi," said Ryan, holding his hand out to Katie. "My name is Ryan Coates. What's yours?"

"K-Katie," she stammered. She quickly reached out and shook his hand, putting it back into her lap because she was shaking.

"Katie, it's nice to meet you. Do you live in our building?"

Before Katie could answer, Sarah stepped between them and pulled Ryan toward the other end of the couch. "I haven't talked to you all day," said Sarah. "We can talk while Tennison and Karen—oops—I mean Katie look at the magazines."

"That's Sarah's boyfriend," whispered Tennison. "His father is a big-time attorney here in Chicago, and they are extremely rich. They live in the penthouse."

"He's cute," said Katie.

"Yes, he is the most handsome guy at our school. All the girls are in love with him."

"Sarah and Ryan are girlfriend and boyfriend?"

"I guess. I know Sarah likes him a lot, but I don't know whether he likes her as much as she likes him. They do spend a lot of time together, though."

Katie kept glancing over at Ryan while she and Tennison continued to talk. Once, she saw Ryan glimpse at her and smile. It made her blush.

"Katie."

Katie looked and saw her mother standing by the concierge desk. "Katie, it's time for you to say goodbye to your friends. The moving van has arrived, and I need your help unpacking," said her mother.

Katie handed the magazine back to Tennison. "Thank you for letting me join you."

"You're welcome," said Tennison. "Let's get together tomorrow."

"I'd like that," said Katie. She turned toward Sarah and Ryan. "Sarah and Ryan, it was a pleasure to meet you too."

"Sure thing, Karen," said Sarah, her voice cold and menacing.

"See you around," said Ryan. He gave Katie a smile that formed a perfect heart. She had never seen a smile so warm and welcoming. She thought she would faint as the blood rushed from her head to her feet.

As Katie and her mother rode the elevator to their condo, Katie grabbed her mother's hand and asked, "Can we go shopping tomorrow? I need some new clothes."

"You look fine," said her mother.

"But I need some new school clothes," she begged. "And there is a big dance coming up. Can I go? I'll need a new dress."

"We'll see. Right now, let's go unpack."

⤝⤞

CHAPTER 4

Katie woke early. Sunlight streamed through her bedroom window because her mother hadn't had time to hang the curtains. She sat on the side of her bed and looked around the bedroom stacked high with moving boxes and bedroom furniture that hadn't found a permanent home.

She had stayed up until after midnight helping her mother unpack boxes, make beds, and straighten the furniture, but the room still looked like it hadn't been touched. Boxes, clothes, and stuff were everywhere.

She went to her suitcase and took out a clean pair of jeans and a light blue blouse. She didn't take the time to shower or brush her teeth because she knew her day would be spent cleaning and unpacking the boxes strewn around the condo like Lego blocks.

She thought if she hurried, dressed, and unpacked all the boxes in her room, her mom would take her shopping for new clothes.

She opened one of the moving boxes from the stack in the corner of the room. Inside were all her stuffed animals. She carefully removed each animal from the box and gently sat them on her bed. She loved her stuffed animal collection because her father had bought most of them for her. One of the teddy bears was dressed like a pirate, another wore a baseball uniform, and another had on a tutu and looked like a ballerina. But her favorite bear was the one that was dressed in mountain hiking gear: a backpack, khaki shorts, and hiking boots. Her father had named the bear Hillary in honor of Sir Edmond Hillary, the first man to climb Mt. Everest—the tallest mountain on Earth. She missed her dad.

Once the box was empty, she pulled it apart and laid it flat on the floor with the other folded boxes. She reached for another box, but before she could open it, her door swung open with a big thud, and Mikey walked in. "I'm hungry," he said.

"Go to the kitchen and fix yourself some cereal," replied Katie as she opened the box.

"I don't know how."

"You know how. Get the box of cereal you like best, dump it in a bowl, get the milk out of the refrigerator, and pour it on the cereal. Oh, and don't forget a spoon. How difficult can it be?"

"I want you to help me," he whined.

"Mikey, do it yourself. I'm busy. I want to finish unpacking. I want Mom to take me to the store and buy me some new clothes."

"Why do you need new clothes? You look fine to me."

"You wouldn't understand if I told you," said Katie.

"Yes, I would."

"All right, I'll tell you. I need new clothes for school. The clothes I have aren't cool—they are so last year. My clothes are outdated because Mom hasn't taken me shopping since Dad died."

"Who said your clothes aren't cool? I like them."

"Mikey, you're too little to understand what's cool and what's not," said Katie. Now go to the kitchen and fix yourself some breakfast. I'm busy."

"I want you to help me," said Mikey loudly. "Mom says you're supposed to help me when I can't do things. You're the oldest."

"Hold down your voice," whispered Katie as she put her finger to her lips. "You're going to wake up Mom, and you know how tired she is. She needs her rest."

"I don't care," said Mikey even louder. "You're my big sister, and you're supposed to help me."

"What's going on in there?" asked Katie's mom as she entered the room. Her eyes were red from lack of sleep, and her hair looked like the nest of some berserk barn swallow. She had on her old pink flannel pajamas and her white bunny slippers. Katie's dad had given her the slippers as a joke on one of her birthdays. Her dad had always liked to give one serious gift and one silly gift on people's birthdays. It always made him laugh when they were opened. "I said, what's going on in here?"

"Nothing," replied Katie.

"Why is your brother screaming his head off if nothing is happening?"

"He wanted me to fix him some breakfast," said Katie.

"Then why didn't you go to the kitchen and fix it for him?" asked Katie's mom. She folded her arms across her chest and scowled at Katie.

"Mom, Mikey is seven years old. He can certainly pour his own cereal."

"That's not the point, Katie," countered her mother. "The point is, we all must work together to make this family work. And right now, you're not pulling your share of the load. Why couldn't you stop what you were doing and help him with his breakfast?"

Katie felt her chin quiver and tears well up in her eyes. "Because I thought if I finished with the unpacking, you and I could shop for new clothes."

"Well, you thought wrong. I won't buy you new clothes until you can prove that you can help me with your little brother. He's younger than you and needs his big sister to help him when he needs it. I can't do everything around here."

"Who's going to help me when I need it?" asked Katie as she fought back tears.

"Don't talk back to me, young lady," said her mother. "I don't have time to argue with you right now. I'm tired and need to get the apartment in order before I start work tomorrow. I need you to cooperate and help me."

"Okay, Mom," whispered Katie in defeat.

"Take your brother into the kitchen and fix him some breakfast while I shower and dress. Can you at least do that?"

"Yes." Katie frowned.

Mikey moved over to his mother's side and smiled back at Katie. A devilish gleam in his eye seemed to say "I beat you again."

Katie grabbed Mikey by the arm and pulled him toward the kitchen. He refused to move his feet. Katie had to drag him across the hardwood floor in his socks like a sleigh.

As they reached the kitchen, her cell phone rang in her back pocket. Katie let go of Mikey's arm and looked at the screen. It was a number she didn't know. She pushed the button on her phone. "Hello?"

"Is Katie there," said a boy.

"This is Katie."

"Hi, Katie, this is Ryan Coates. We met in the lobby yesterday. You were with Sarah and Tennison."

"How could I forget?" said Katie as she choked on her words. Her mouth was dry, and her heart was beating like a drum. "How did you get my phone number?"

"I got your phone number from Godfrey, who works at the front desk. He and I are friends. Even though he's not supposed to give out private cell phone numbers, he does it for me sometimes," chuckled Ryan. "I told him it was an emergency."

"What's the emergency?" asked Katie.

"I was wondering if you want to go to the beach with us today. Tennison, Sarah, and I will leave about eleven o'clock and have a hot dog at Navy Pier before we head to the beach. Do you want to join us?"

Katie couldn't believe her ears. Had the best-looking boy in the whole wide world just asked her to go to the beach for the afternoon? Had she heard him correctly? "Excuse me," she said. She coughed as she tried to get some moisture back in her mouth.

"I asked you if you wanted to go to the beach today?"

"Let me check with my mom," replied Katie. She placed her phone on the kitchen counter and ran to her mother's bedroom.

Her mother was still in the shower. Katie opened the bathroom door and shouted, "Mom, can I go to the beach with some friends?"

"What did you say?" asked her mother as she peeked from around the shower curtain.

"Ryan asked me to go to the beach. Can I go?"

"You know better than to ask that question," said her mother as gray-white steam from the shower circled her head like a cloud. "We have to unpack."

"But, Mom, he's the best-looking boy I've ever met."

"I don't care if he looks like Tanner Buchanan. You can't go."

Katie felt like someone had dropped a ton of bricks on her head. This was one of the most popular guys she'd ever met, and her mother wouldn't allow her to be friends with him. It made her mad.

She needed to meet friends before school started, but her mother kept her from making any.

She stomped back to the kitchen. Each of her heavy footsteps echoed off the hardwood floors like blows from a hammer. When she reached the kitchen, her mouth fell open, her heart stopped, and she almost fainted. Her phone wasn't on the countertop where she had left it.

She looked at Mikey. He was holding it as he sat at the table. "What happened to my phone?"

"It was on the counter. I hung it up." He grinned.

"How could you do that to me, Mikey," said Katie. "Why do you want to ruin my life?"

Mikey didn't say a thing. He walked to the refrigerator door, opened it, and took out the milk carton. He then went to the cupboard and retrieved a box of cereal.

"Mikey, why did you hang up my phone?" Her shoulders slumped, and her knees started to shake.

"Things happen," he said.

Katie picked up her phone off the kitchen table and tried to call Ryan back, but a recorded voice said, "This number is private."

Frantically, she dialed the front desk. A voice on the other end said, "Front desk, how may I assist you."

"Godfrey?" asked Katie. "This is Katie Sparrow in 5406. Can you give me the Ryan Coates's cellphone number?"

"Sorry, Ms. Sparrow, I can't give out other tenants' telephone numbers. It is against building policy."

"Please," begged Katie.

"Sorry, but I can't. That would break the rules, and I could lose my job."

"Okay," she whispered. "I understand."

She realized her life was over. Any chance of making friends with Ryan, Sarah, and Tennison was destroyed. She knew Ryan would never talk to her again because he would think she intentionally hung up on him. She bit her lower lip. What was she going to do?

CHAPTER 5

Katie spent the rest of the day helping her mother unpack boxes, roll out rugs, and move furniture into its final spot. She wished Ryan would call her back the whole time she worked, but he didn't.

What would she say the next time they met, she wondered. He won't even talk to me for hanging up on him. Her heart sank in her chest, and a new sadness settled over her like a sticky, warm summer's day. She felt miserable.

"What's wrong with you?" asked her mother as she sat down on the couch that she and Katie had just slid into place against the living room wall.

Katie pulled the rest of the clear plastic wrap off the couch and sat down beside her mother. She rubbed her sore arms. "Nothing," she lied.

"What is it, Katie? I know something is wrong. I can see it in your eyes. You're not acting like your normal, happy self."

"I feel sad, that's all. I miss Camden. I miss Alpine. And I miss Daddy."

"You'll make new friends," replied her mother. "You've only been here two days, and I'm sure there are a lot of girls your age in the neighborhood. What about the two girls you met yesterday in the lobby? They seemed nice."

"Not really," said Katie. "Tennison was nice, but Sarah's not friendly at all. I think she hates me."

"What made you think that?"

"I don't know, I could just feel it." Katie didn't want to tell her mother about the nasty things Sarah had said about her while they looked at fashion magazines. Just thinking about the cruel things

Sarah had said made her feel even worse than she already felt. She looked down at her old clothes.

"I am sure Sarah doesn't hate you. She doesn't know you yet."

"I don't think getting to know me will help," said Katie. When Mikey walked into the room carrying his toy dump truck, Katie was ready to tell her mother about what Sarah had said about her clothes.

"Mom, I'm hungry," he whined.

"Let me unpack a few more boxes, and then I'll fix us some dinner," replied Mom with a heavy sigh. "I need to get as much done tonight as possible because I must start work in the morning. After dinner, your new nanny will come by to meet you."

"But I'm hungry now," said Mikey. "I can't wait."

"Get an apple out of the refrigerator."

"Mom," whined Mikey loudly.

"Okay, I'll get us something to eat. Katie, continue to unpack while I go in the kitchen and see what I can scare up for us to eat."

Katie looked at her mother in disbelief. She wondered why she always caved into Mikey and did everything he wanted her to do. Maybe it was because he looked so much like their dad. Whatever it was, Katie could tell that he was Mom's favorite and that she was taking up space in the family unit—sitting on the edge of the family now that her father was dead, invisible to her mother except when she needed someone to yell at or do chores.

Katie stood and looked for another box to unload. She watched her mother walk into the kitchen. What must I do to get Mom to notice me again?

"Can I help you unload boxes?" asked Mikey.

"Go away, Mikey. I don't need your help. Go help Mom in the kitchen." She felt anger swell in her chest, and her cheeks turned a fiery red. She also felt herself resenting her little brother because her mom liked him best.

"But I want to help."

"Get out of here!" screamed Katie. "You're nothing but a pest."

"What's going on in there?" called Mom from the kitchen.

"Katie yelled at me and called me a bad name," said Mikey.

"Katie, leave your brother alone and unpack the boxes as I ask. Can you do what I ask just once?"

It wasn't any use trying anymore. She couldn't do anything right in her mother's eyes. *Am I the pest?* She wished she were back in Alpine, Utah, and over at Camden's house baking cookies with her mom. She wished Camden's mother were her mother because she was the coolest mother in town.

Katie's thoughts were broken by the buzzing of a cell phone. She had left her phone on the counter in the kitchen. Her heart skipped a beat. *I hope it's Ryan calling me back.* "I'll get it," she screamed. She rushed to get her phone, but her mother had already answered it before she could retrieve it from its spot on the counter. It wasn't her cell phone buzzing but her mother's.

Katie watched in silence as her mother talked on the phone. Mom hung up the phone and turned to Katie. "Hurry and brush your hair. That was Godfrey at the front desk. He said that Mrs. Sanchez is here and will arrive at our apartment in a few minutes."

"Who's Mrs. Sanchez?" asked Mikey.

"She's your new nanny," replied Mom as she washed her hands in the sink and wiped them on her jeans. She grabbed Mikey by the arm and pulled him to her. She ran her fingers through his thick, tangled hair like a comb. It made little difference to the matted mess on top of his head.

Katie raced to the bathroom and ran a brush through her hair. She was able to get out a few knots and tangles when she heard a knock at the front door.

"Katie, can you get the door?" called Mom from the kitchen.

Katie went to the door and swung it open. In the hallway was a heavyset lady with straight black hair and streaks of gray running through it. Her eyes were a deep brown, and her skin was the color of coffee. Her nose was broad and looked like someone had cobbled it onto her face with a hammer. She smiled at Katie with a set of stained teeth that protruded between lips that were covered by ruby-red lipstick. She wore a brightly colored skirt and a fluffy white, sleeveless blouse. On her feet were a pair of black shoes with extra thick soles, the kind of shoes you see nurses and hairdressers wear. The kind of shoes that are built for comfort and not for looks. Katie couldn't help but stare at this strange, matronly-looking person standing in the hallway. "Come in," she finally offered.

"Thank you, señorita," said the nanny in a thick Spanish accent. "Es your mother, Señorita Sparrow, at home?"

"Yes, she is. Please come in, and I will get her for you."

"Muchas gracias."

Katie hurried toward the kitchen where Mom was putting the final touches to Mikey's unruly hair that she finally got to hold in place with a dab of spit. "Mom, the nanny is here," she announced.

"I know, Katie. I heard the knock." Mom grabbed Mikey's hand and pulled him toward the living room. Mikey twisted free from her grasp and ran toward his bedroom. "Mikey, get back here right now."

Mikey laughed and slammed the door to his room.

"Katie, would you please go get your brother?"

"You know he won't listen to me."

"Just get him, Katie, while I talk to Mrs. Sanchez."

"Okay," grumbled Katie. She went to Mikey's room and opened the door. "Come on, Mikey, Mom wants us to meet our new nanny."

"I don't want a nanny," he said stubbornly.

"Neither do I, but we've got to do what Mom says," continued Katie. "Be a grown-up boy and come on."

"Why can't grandma come to Chicago and be our nanny?" asked Mikey.

"Because she lives in Utah, and all her friends are there."

"All my friends are in Utah too, but here I am in Chicago. Why can't she leave her friends like we did and move to Chicago?"

"Don't ask those kinds of questions. You know Grandma can't move to Chicago. Now, come on."

Reluctantly, Mikey took Katie's hand, and they walked toward the living room.

✄

CHAPTER 6

"Get up, Katie," Mom called. "Mrs. Sanchez will be here in a few minutes, and I have to go to work."

Katie sat up in bed and wiped the sleep from her eyes. "Can't you stay home today? I need to go shopping for new clothes."

"You know better than that," replied Mom. "I must start my new job today. I will leave some money on the kitchen counter, and you, Mikey, and Mrs. Sanchez can go shopping."

Katie scrambled out of bed and followed her mother down the hall toward the kitchen. "I don't want to go shopping with Mrs. Sanchez. I want to go shopping with you."

"Katie, stop acting like a little girl. I need you to grow up and act your age. I must go to work. I'm already late." Mom slipped a piece of dry, burnt toast in her mouth. It crunched noisily in her mouth as she chewed it. "Mrs. Sanchez will need your help with Mikey. You know how stubborn he is around new people."

"I'm not sure I like Mrs. Sanchez," sighed Katie.

"She seems nice to me," said Mom as she continued to chew her toast. "You'll like her once you get to know her."

"I don't think so. She looks mean."

Before Mom could reply, there was a knock on the front door. "That must be Mrs. Sanchez. Katie, can you please get the door? I forgot to give her a key to the apartment last night. I will give it to her today."

"But, Mom, I'm in my pajamas."

"I'm sure Mrs. Sanchez doesn't mind seeing you in your pajamas."

Katie reluctantly went to the door and swung it open. She gasped. Not only was Mrs. Sanchez standing at the door, but so was Ryan. She hurriedly pushed the door halfway closed and peered around the edge.

"It's me, señorita, Mrs. Sanchez. Can I come in?"

"I know it's you, Mrs. Sanchez, but I'm not dressed."

"And it's me, Ryan," he said with a sheepish grin.

"I know you too," said Katie.

Mrs. Sanchez pushed her way past Katie and headed to the kitchen. Ryan remained in the hallway. He put his hands in the pockets of her shorts and smiled at Katie. She wasn't sure if she should let him see her in her pajamas or let him stand in the hallway. She finally decided to let him stand in the hallway.

"Since you hung up on me yesterday, I decided to see if you would talk to me in person," he said.

"That wasn't me yesterday," said Katie. She felt her face flush with embarrassment. "My little brother hung up on you. He's only seven, and he's really a pest."

"That's okay," said Ryan. "I thought I would come by and see if you wanted to go to Navy Pier with us today. We'll ride the Ferris wheel and then go to the beach."

Before she could answer, her mother was at the door. "Who's this?" asked Mom.

"Mom, this is Ryan. Ryan, this is my mother, Dr. Sparrow."

"Good morning, Dr. Sparrow," said Ryan politely. He stuck out his hand to shake hers. "I stopped by to see if Katie could go to Navy Pier with a bunch of us from the building today?"

"I'm sorry, Ryan, Katie has to stay here and help the new nanny tend to her little brother." Mom squeezed past Katie and into the hallway before heading to the elevators. "Ryan, it was nice to meet you," she called as she pushed the down button on the elevator bank. "I hope to see you again soon."

"I'm sorry you can't go with us," said Ryan. "We'll miss you."

"Me too," said Katie.

"Maybe some other time." He took his hands out of his pockets, turned around, and headed toward the elevators.

"Sure," whispered Katie. She watched him step into the elevator and disappear inside. She knew in her heart he would never ask her to go anywhere again. Once again, Mikey was getting in the way and keeping her from living her own life. She closed the door and sat cross-legged in the middle of the floor.

Why is life so unfair? Why was she being punished for her father's death? It wasn't her fault he had gotten sick. Why was everyone blaming her for everything that went wrong? She started to cry.

"Why the big tears, señorita?" asked Mrs. Sanchez.

"You wouldn't understand."

"Just 'cause I speak with an accent doesn't mean I don't understand when a girl's heart is breaking," said Mrs. Sanchez. She sat down on the floor next to Katie and put her fleshy brown arm around her shoulders. "Tell Auntie Maria what the problem is."

"I don't want to talk about it," sobbed Katie. "Please leave me alone."

"Now, now. It's best to talk to someone when you have a problem. If you don't talk about it, it will fester like a sore and get worse. I know what I'm talking about. I was once a girl your age."

It was hard for Katie to believe this matronly woman was ever a young girl. *And what could she possibly know of how hard it was to be a young girl these days?* "You wouldn't understand."

"When I was a young girl in Mexico, I lived with my mother, father, and three sisters in a little town outside Obregon. My father was a farmer. He didn't make much money, but we had a casa, and there was always plenty of food on the table and clothes on our backs. We were a happy familia. One day, while my papa was cutting hay on our old gray tractor, the mower jammed with alfalfa. He got off the tractor and pulled on the tangled plants until they came loose, and when it did, the blade of the mower came down on his arm and cut him very badly. He took off his shirt and wrapped it tightly around his arm to stop the bleeding. My mother rushed him to the doctor in hopes of saving my father's arm and his life. The doctor looked at my father's arm and decided it was too badly mangled, and he would have to remove it to save my father's life, so he did. My father could not work the farm anymore with just one arm. We had to move from the country to Mexico City where my father worked as a night watchman at one of the many automobile assembly plants surrounding the city.

"The job didn't pay very well, so my mother and older sister had to find jobs too. We lived in a small apartment on the city's west side, a part of town the locals called a slum. There were many days and nights when there wasn't enough food for all of us, and we had to go to bed hungry. And we had to wear our clothes until they fell off our backs. I was fourteen years old when this happened, and I thought my world had collapsed. I was embarrassed by my father and his one arm and my mother, who worked in one of the factories. I was humiliated that my sister had to work washing other people's clothes in a laundry. I was ashamed of our tiny, run-down apartment and that we had to wear shabby clothes. I hated my life.

"One day, while I was walking the streets looking for soda pop bottles I could return to the store for the deposit money, I saw a boy that looked to be my age standing in front of one of the shop windows. He was tall with brown eyes and a mischievous smile. He was well-dressed, so she knew his family had money. He was the most handsome boy I had ever seen. I stood there in the street as if my feet were stuck in cement. I just stared at him. I couldn't move.

"He must have seen my reflection in the shop window because he turned around and looked at me. I wanted to crawl into a hole so he wouldn't see my shabby clothes and the holes in my shoes. He kept staring at me, and I bowed my head so I didn't have to see his face. He walked toward me, and I thought my heart would stop as he did. When he reached where I stood, he said, 'What are you looking at?' My mouth was so dry I couldn't open my mouth to speak. The more I stared into his brown eyes, the more I wanted to melt into the street. Finally, I croaked, 'I thought you were someone I knew, but obviously, you're not. I'm sorry for staring at you.'

"He smiled back at me and said, 'That's all right, I am flattered that you thought you knew me.' He asked my name, and he told me his name was Juan. We talked for a few minutes, and I hoped he wasn't judging me because of my sad clothes and scuffed shoes. He didn't seem to notice. We just stood there in the street and talked. I knew at that moment what it was like to fall in love. I wanted to reach out and touch his soft brown skin and run my fingers through his tangled black hair.

"He said he wanted to see me again. I told him I would meet him at the same shop the next day. And for the next two weeks, we met at the shop. We walked the streets as we held each other's hands and talked about soccer, books, and the most recent American movies. He told me he was from a wealthy family in Mexico City and that he wanted to grow up to become a rich businessman. He said he wanted to marry me, and we would live in a big house in one of the rich neighborhoods.

"Then it happened. His father passed us in his big fancy car as we walked. He stopped and pulled over to the side of the road. He ordered Juan to get in the car. He told Juan to stop mingling with a poor local girl, and if he knew what was best for him, he would never see me again. I saw tears in Juan's eyes as he walked to his father's car and slid into the back seat. He weakly waved at me as the car sped away. My heart split in two as I watched the car drive away. I knew I would never again love anyone as much as I loved Juan. I knew I would never be able to love anyone else as deeply as I loved him at that moment."

"Did you ever see Juan again?" asked Katie. She had listened with interest to Mrs. Sanchez's story and had to dry her tears on the sleeve of her pajamas. She looked up into Mrs. Sanchez's dark brown eyes and could see in her eyes the dreamy state her memories had carried her to.

"No, we never saw each other again," sighed Mrs. Sanchez. "I'm sure he is a highly successful businessman back in Mexico."

"That's sad," said Katie.

"When I was eighteen years old, I applied for a work visa in America to be a nanny for a wealthy family in Chicago. I've been here ever since. I married a nice man here many years ago. We have six children. Most of them are grown now and have families of their own."

"Do you still miss Juan?" asked Katie.

"Sometimes I wonder what my life would have been like if he and I had fallen in love and gotten married, but I wouldn't trade my children and husband for all the money in Mexico. So you see, Katie, I know something about broken hearts."

"Yes, you do," replied Katie with a grin. She reached out and gave Mrs. Sanchez a hug.

"Now, can you tell me what is bothering you?"

"I don't have any friends here in Chicago," said Katie, "and the kids that I have met don't like me. They say I don't fit in because of my old clothes."

"The boy that was just here at the door must have thought you fit in, or he wouldn't have asked you to go to Navy Pier."

"Ryan? Oh, he already has a girlfriend. And every girl in the neighborhood is in love with him. He's too good-looking to be friends with someone like me."

"You never know," said Mrs. Sanchez. She stood and pulled Katie to her feet. "Why don't you help me with breakfast? Then we can take your brother for a walk. We can even walk down to Navy Pier if you like."

At that moment, Mrs. Sanchez didn't look like a matronly, mean nanny. In Katie's eyes, she looked perfect. "Thank you, Mrs. Sanchez."

"Call me Auntie Maria."

CHAPTER 7

The next few days passed slowly as Katie spent her time straightening her room and helping Mikey unpack his boxes. She even pitched in and helped Mrs. Sanchez clean and organize the condo. She only left the building twice during this time, and both were trips to the grocery store with Mrs. Sanchez.

She didn't see much of her mother because she was in bed asleep by the time her mother got home from work. Katie only saw her for a few minutes each morning at breakfast before her mother darted out the door.

Even though she stayed busy, she was lonely and sad. She wished Ryan would call her back and ask her to join him at Navy Pier, but her cell phone remained silent and didn't ring. At night, she sat alone in her bedroom, listened to music, and wished she were back in Alpine playing video games with Camden. Each day seemed to pass more slowly than the day before. She wished she were anywhere other than Chicago. She wanted her old life back.

One night, as Katie sat on her bed with her headset on and listened to music, her mother entered the room. Mom tapped her on the shoulder, pulled one of the earphones off her ear, and said, "Katie, can we talk?"

Katie removed the other earphone from her ear and looked up at her mother. "Mom, I don't want to talk right now. I'm listening to my music."

"I think we need to talk," continued Mom.

Katie turned around and faced her mother. "Okay, what do you want to talk about?"

"I want to talk about us. It's been a long time since you and I have talked." Mom sat down next to Katie, put her hands on her knees, and looked Katie in the eyes.

"No, Mom, I've been talking to you, but you haven't listened. You're always too busy to listen to me. Your new job, the move to Chicago, and pampering Mikey have pushed me into the background. I'm invisible to you. You haven't seen or listened to me since Daddy died."

Her mother rubbed her hands together and then tugged nervously at the sleeve of her shirt. "You're right," she whispered. "How can I make it up to you?"

"I think it's too late now, Mom," said Katie.

"It's never too late for a mother and daughter to make up and patch up their relationship. Surely, there is something I can do to let you know how much I love you and how sorry I am for the way I've acted the past few months."

Katie watched as tears formed in the corner of her mother's eyes, and one fell and rolled down her cheek. She felt terrible for making her mother cry. She put her hand on her mother's hand and said, "Don't cry, Mom."

"I know I haven't been the same since your father died, and I'm sorry for that, but I thought by me staying busy, the pain would go away quicker. Now, I realize I've made things worse."

Katie didn't say a word. She just stared at her mother and watched as more tears fell and trickled down her cheeks and rolled off her chin.

"I miss your father so much," continued her mother, "and I know nothing will ever fill the emptiness and this void I have in my chest. I know I shouldn't let my sadness get in the way of our relationship and keep us from sharing the bond we once had. Please let me make it up to you."

Katie nodded her head in agreement and said, "Okay, Mom."

"I know what we can do," said her mother as a smile crept across her face. "Let's go shopping on Saturday. We can have lunch at a nice restaurant and then buy some things for your new bedroom."

"I would rather shop for clothes," said Katie.

"You don't want some new sheets or pillowcases for your room?"

"Mom, I have plenty of sheets and pillowcases. School will be starting soon, and I need some new clothes."

"You're right," said her mother. "Let's get you some new clothes. That sounds like a great idea. Let's do it. It's a date."

Katie reached over and hugged her mother around the neck. "Oh, thank you. Thank you so much."

Katie couldn't wait for Saturday to arrive. She felt happy inside, and everything around her seemed bright and cheerful. Chicago didn't seem like such a bad place after all, and for the first time in a long time, she enjoyed playing with Mikey.

On Friday night, Katie had difficulty falling asleep because of her excitement. She lay in bed and tossed and turned as she thought about spending the day with her mother and thinking about which new clothes she would buy. She was also thrilled about having her mother alone without Mikey or Mrs. Sanchez around. Her thoughts kept swirling around inside her head like a snowstorm. She was too keyed up to sleep but finally drifted off to dreamland around midnight.

She woke the next morning to the sound of the television set. She rubbed her eyes and looked around. Sunlight streamed through her windows, and she could see it would be a beautiful day.

She jumped out of bed and ran into the living room. She couldn't wait to start the day. Shopping with her mother made her pulse race, and her heart pounded rapidly in her chest. This would be the day that started a new chapter with her and her mother.

Mikey was on the couch watching cartoons and eating a bowl of chocolate chip ice cream. "Does Mom know you're eating ice cream for breakfast," asked Katie.

Mikey stuck out his tongue at Katie and shook his head back and forth. "No, Mom doesn't know I'm eating ice cream for breakfast," he crowed.

"Well, when she comes out of her bedroom, she will be very mad at you. You know you're not supposed to eat ice cream for breakfast."

"Mom won't be coming out of her bedroom," said Mikey defiantly.

"What do you mean she won't be coming out of her bedroom? Is she sick, or did you lock her in her bedroom?"

"No." Mikey grinned mischievously. "She left about ten minutes ago. She said she had an emergency at the clinic and had to get down there as soon as possible. She left a note for you on the kitchen counter."

Katie couldn't believe her ears. *Did Mikey say her mother had just left to go to the clinic? That was impossible. She and her mother had a shopping date! Surely, her mother hadn't forgotten.* She ran to the kitchen and picked up the note. It was written in her mother's large, broad strokes and said, "Dear Katie, I am so sorry about today. I must go to the clinic for a few hours. One of my patients needs an emergency root canal. I will be home as soon as possible. Sorry. Love, Mom."

Katie felt her legs turn to Jell-O, and she began to shake. *This can't be happening*, she thought. She let the note slip from her fingers and float gently to the floor. She kicked the kitchen counter and screamed.

"I told you," yelled Mikey from the living room.

"Be quiet, Mikey," screamed Katie.

"Mom said you were to watch me until Mrs. Sanchez arrives."

"I'm not waiting here for Mrs. Sanchez," said Katie defiantly. She bent over, picked up the note off the floor, and tore it into a hundred little pieces. "If Mom's not shopping with me, I'll go alone."

"You can't go shopping, Katie. You don't have any money."

"I have the money Dad left me and the money Grandma gave me just before we moved. I'll go to Michigan Avenue by myself."

"You had better not. You know Mom will get mad at you for leaving the condo without her."

"When did you ever care what Mom thinks? You never listen to her. You never do what she says, so why should I?"

"I'm telling."

"I don't care. I'm going shopping."

Katie ran to her room and jumped in the shower. Within minutes, she was dressed and ready to go out. As she walked toward the front door, she began to have second thoughts about leaving the condo. She didn't feel as confident as she had a few minutes earlier. She stood and stared at the front door.

She knew her mother would be furious with her for leaving Mikey alone, but she figured if her mother cared that much, she would have stayed home and gone shopping with her.

She took a deep breath, opened the door, and entered the hallway. The last thing she heard before closing the door was Mikey's voice in the background, "You're dead meat, Katie. I wouldn't want to be you when Mom gets home."

Katie walked through the revolving door of the condo building and stepped into the warm sunshine. The sunshine felt like a warm blanket on her shoulders. She had gone to Michigan Avenue several times with Mrs. Sanchez, but right now, she wasn't sure she could find it alone. She looked down the sidewalk to the left and right and then decided to go left, turn left again, and walk west on Grand Avenue.

She took a deep breath to help gain courage and then started to walk down McClurg Court Street.

"Kathy, is that you?" said a voice from behind her. She turned around, and there, coming out of the condo building, was Sarah.

"My name is Katie."

"Yes, I remember—Katie, the country girl," said Sarah with an impish grin.

"No, it's just plain Katie."

"I can see from your country clothes that you are just plain Katie," said Sarah.

Katie's cheeks turned a bright red with anger. She didn't like Sarah, and she felt like hitting someone for the first time in her life. "Hello, Sarah."

"Does your mother know you've left the farm alone this morning? Isn't a country girl like you afraid to be out in the big city all on your own? Aren't you afraid a bogeyman might get you?"

Katie clenched her fists. She knew if she didn't get out of there soon, she would end up doing something she would regret later. "Sarah, you look cute today."

"I know. I look cute every day."

Katie couldn't take anymore; she turned and walked away.

"Where are you going, Country Katie?" called Sarah.

Katie didn't say a word. She just kept walking. She felt a hand grab her shoulder and pulled her around. "I asked you a question, Country Katie," demanded Sarah. "Don't ever walk away from me without answering my questions, do you understand? While you live here in Chicago and in my condo building, you had better learn to play by my rules, Country Katie, or I'll ruin you. I'll ensure you never have a friend here and that no one in the building will ever talk to you. Do you understand me?"

Katie nodded her head. She was humiliated, ashamed, and embarrassed. She wanted to cry but wasn't about to give Sarah the satisfaction of seeing her cry. She also wanted to yell at Sarah and call her names, but she knew it wouldn't do any good. It never helps to call people names; she knew it would only worsen things. She bit her lower lip and stared at Sarah.

"Country Katie, you had better stay out of my way, and I had better never see you hanging around Ryan. He's my boyfriend, and I don't want you anywhere around him."

"I think he can decide for himself who he wants to hang with. He seems like a smart boy, and I'm sure he doesn't need someone like you telling him who he can be seen with. You're not his mother, are you?"

"I'm warning you, Country Katie, you'd better watch yourself."

"If you're finished, I need to go now," said Katie calmly.

"Don't you need your babysitter with you?"

"I don't need anyone." Katie turned around and walked away. When she had taken a few steps, she peeked over her shoulder to see if Sarah was still standing there, but she was nowhere to be seen. Katie took a deep breath and kept walking. When she reached the corner, she turned left on Grand Avenue and headed west toward Michigan Avenue. It was still early, and few people were on the street.

When she reached Michigan Avenue, she climbed the metal stairs that led from Grand Avenue up to the stores. She stood at the top of the stairs and looked around. There were stores as far as her eyes could see in both directions. *Where should I start?* she wondered.

Slowly, she walked down the street, staring into the windows at the beautiful clothes. The stores were so big, much bigger than the stores she had seen in American Fork, Provo, and Salt Lake City, where she and her mother had shopped when they lived in Alpine, and the window displays were so cleverly and artistically arranged that they made the clothes and shoes look even more beautiful.

She walked along the street for almost an hour before she had the courage to enter one of the big stores. When she decided to enter the Water Tower Mall, the sidewalks swarmed with tourists and shoppers. She had to dodge, twist, and turn past the mob of people at the entrance to the mall; but finally, she pushed her way through the revolving door and entered the lobby.

She took the escalator from the lobby to the second floor and entered the Gap store. It was filled with trendy jeans, shirts, blouses, sweaters, and tops. Over at one of the tables stacked high with jeans was a group of girls that looked to be her age. Hesitantly, she walked toward them, but they turned and looked at her just before she reached them. One of the girls, a blond with dark-blue eyes, pointed at her, whispered something to the girl next to her and pointed at Katie. They both started to laugh. Katie was sure they were making fun of her old clothes. She wished she could turn into an ant and crawl away, but she stood there as her cheeks turned a fiery red. *Why does everyone make fun of me?*

The girls continued to giggle as they walked past her. She stood there and didn't dare move. She wished Camden was there with her.

There was a tap on her shoulder as she stood there frozen in place like one of the mannequins thinking about Camden. She swung around expecting to see the blond girls again, but instead of the blond, there stood Ryan smiling at her. She didn't know what to do. Finally, she eked out a weak "Hello, Ryan."

"Hi, Katie, what are you doing out here by yourself? You need to be here with a friend. Michigan Avenue is more fun with a friend."

"I don't have any friends here in Chicago," she replied.

"I know Tennison likes you," continued Ryan with a toothy grin. "And I'm one of your friends."

Katie blushed. "I didn't think you would ever talk to me again after what happened last week."

"Don't worry about that. I'm your friend. Do you mind if I shop with you?" asked Ryan.

"I'd like that very much," stammered Katie. "But Sarah told me never to talk to you again."

"She doesn't choose my friends," said Ryan.

"Good," said Katie.

"Then let's get started. What are you looking for?"

"Some new clothes."

Ryan touched her elbow and guided her toward the display tables. Together, they looked at the jeans. Katie found a pair she liked and went to the dressing room to try them on. She liked them but decided she would get Ryan's opinion. She stepped out of the dressing room and stood in front of the mirror.

"Wow, you look great," said Ryan.

"Do you think so?"

"Yes, I do. You look good in them."

Katie bought the jeans, and for the next few hours, she and Ryan walked through the mall together. She bought several new tops and a denim skirt. As they shopped, he told her about Chicago, school, and the sports he was involved in. She told him about Utah, Camden, and her dad. They talked and talked as if they had been friends forever. He made her feel important, and she liked him because he made her laugh. She felt happy for the first time in a long time.

"Do you want to get something to eat?" he asked.

"Yes, I'm very hungry. I left the house without eating breakfast."

"I know just the spot."

They walked west on Delaware Street and stopped at Johnny Rockets hamburger shop. They went inside and sat at one of the booths. They both ordered a hamburger, fries, and a chocolate shake. Their orders arrived when Katie heard someone call her name.

She looked over the top of the booth, and her mother stood at the doorway. She stood there with her hands on her hips and a glare on her face.

"Katie, what are you doing?" said her mother when she reached the booth. Everyone in the restaurant turned and looked in their direction. "I've been looking for you for two hours. I even called the police. You know better than to leave the house without someone."

Katie was embarrassed. She felt everyone's eyes boring through her. She looked at Ryan for help. He smiled at her and winked.

"She was with me the whole time, Dr. Sparrow," said Ryan politely and respectfully. His voice was clear and strong.

"And who are you?" asked Mom.

"I'm Ryan, Dr. Sparrow. We met in the hallway last week. I live in your building."

"And what gave you the right to think you could take my daughter to Michigan Avenue without my permission?"

"I found her on Michigan Avenue by herself and thought she could use a friend."

"You thought wrong, young man," said Mom. "I don't want you to come around my daughter again. Do you understand me?"

"Don't talk to Ryan like that," said Katie as she shot her mother an evil look. "At least he wanted to be with me."

Dr. Sparrow reached into her pant pocket, took out a twenty-dollar bill, and threw it on the table. "This should cover the cost of her hamburger," she said to Ryan. She then reached into the booth and grabbed Katie's arm. "It's time to go, Katie, come on."

Katie looked at Ryan apologetically. She didn't want to leave, but she didn't want to make a bigger scene and pull away from her mother. She slid out of the booth and scooped up her packages. She looked helplessly at Ryan and then followed her mother out of the restaurant. She felt humiliated and embarrassed again. Her mother had just embarrassed her in front of her only friend in Chicago.

For the first time in her life, she disliked her mother very much.

CHAPTER 8

Katie's mother didn't say another word until they reached the condo. When she opened the door, she pushed Katie into the living room and then told her to go to her room. "I'll be in to talk to you just as soon as I've calmed down. You know what you did today was irresponsible. Katie, sometimes you don't think."

Katie put her head down and walked to her room. She shut the door, put down her packages, and then threw herself on her bed. She was so upset she couldn't even cry. She put the pillow over her head and thought about Ryan. In her mind, she could see his unruly blond hair and liquid-blue eyes as they stared at her. She could see his smile and hear his laugh. She knew he liked her, but what would he think of her now? He was certainly too embarrassed by her mother's outburst to ever talk to her again. He would tell everyone about the scene at Johnny Rockets. *How was she going to face anyone again?*

The door opened, and in walked her mother. She sat down on the bed next to Katie. They sat there in silence. Finally, her mother said, "Katie, you scared me today. I didn't know where you were, and you didn't answer your cell phone. I could only imagine the worst. You know better than to leave the condo alone. If you wanted to go shopping, you should have waited for Mrs. Sanchez. She would have gone with you."

"But, Mom, you broke your promise. You said we would go shopping today, and then you went to the clinic. I was so hurt and angry that I just left."

"Just because you were mad doesn't give you the right to go out alone. Chicago is a big city. It's not a little town like Alpine. You could have gotten lost or worse—someone could have hurt you. I couldn't live with myself if someone hurt you."

"I know, but you shouldn't make a promise unless you expect to keep it," whispered Katie.

"I know, sweetie, but it was an emergency, and I had to leave. I'm a doctor, and it's your obligation to go when a patient needs you. You know that."

"Mom, I'm trying to understand, but I don't see how one of your patients can be more important than your daughter. I'm sure you wouldn't have broken a promise to Mikey."

"You have no right to say that. You know I love you as much as Mikey."

"You don't show it," said Katie. She could see in her mother's eyes that her words had stung.

"I'm trying as hard as I can to hold this family together since your father died," said Mom with tears in her eyes.

They sat on the bed in silence. After several minutes, Katie's mother got up and left the room. Soon after, Katie fell asleep. She slept until a knock on the door woke her.

Mrs. Sanchez peeked into the room and said, "Ms. Katie, a young lady is here to see you. She's in the living room."

"Who is it?" asked Katie as she wiped the sleep from her eyes.

"She didn't say."

Katie got off the bed and quickly brushed her hair with the brush she kept on the top of her chest of drawers. She straightened her clothes and followed Mrs. Sanchez into the living room.

Tennison sat on the couch. "Hey, Katie, how are you? I haven't seen you around the past few days, so I thought I would visit and see what you've been up to."

Katie was excited to see Tennison. She sat in one of the over-stuffed chairs beside the couch and said, "I've been stuck in the house the last few days unpacking. You know how it is—you unpack one box, and three more appear. I'm still not finished unpacking."

"We've missed seeing you around," said Tennison.

"Who's we?" asked Katie. She was sure it wasn't Sarah. She was the last person on the face of the Earth that Sarah would ever want to see.

"My brother and me."

"I didn't know you had a brother," replied Katie.

"Yes, I do. He's two years older than I am. His name is Peter. He's really a nice guy when you get to know him."

"I don't remember meeting him."

"You didn't. He's seen you walking around with your little brother and your nanny, Mrs. Sanchez."

"How come he didn't come up and introduce himself?" asked Katie. She grabbed her feet and pulled them underneath her so that she sat cross-legged on the chair.

"He's shy," replied Tennison. "Like me."

Tennison was nervous and played with the hem of her pants while her other hand pulled at a strand of hair.

"It was nice of you to stop by and see me tonight,' said Katie. "It means a lot to me. I wasn't sure if you guys liked me."

"Sure, we like you. Well, Sarah doesn't exactly like you, but I like you. You're nice, and I want to get to know you better."

"I'd like that. Would you like a Coke or something to drink?"

"No, I can't stay long," said Tennison. She acted more nervous than she had just a few minutes before. "Can I ask you a question?"

"Sure."

"Are you going to the big back-to-school dance at Navy Pier at the end of the month? My brother would like to take you if you are," Tennison said shyly.

"Your brother wants to take me to the dance? Why didn't he come and ask me himself?"

"As I said, he's shy."

"Is he too shy to ask me to the dance? If he's that shy, why does he want to go to the dance in the first place?"

"Honestly, he doesn't want to go to the dance. He would rather stay home and play video games, but my mom said he needed to go and wanted me to take him as my date. Do you know how gross it would be to take my brother to the year's biggest dance? That's when I thought of you."

"Why me?"

"I knew you wouldn't have a date yet, and you seemed nice. I just knew you would help me out of this jam. Please help me, please," pleaded Tennison.

Katie stood and paced back and forth in front of the couch. She wanted to go to the dance but didn't want to go with someone she didn't know and with someone who didn't want to take her. And besides, what if Ryan asked her? If she accepted to go to the dance with Peter, she would have to tell Ryan no, and that would break her heart. "I don't know."

"Please, you could go to the dance with us. I'm going with Tyler, and Sarah is going with Ryan."

"Sarah is going to the dance with Ryan?" asked Katie.

"Sure, she is. He asked her to the dance over a month ago."

"He did?"

"Well, he didn't exactly ask her to the dance, but she knows he will."

"How can you be so sure?" asked Katie.

"He'll ask her. She would scratch his eyes out if he didn't ask. Everyone knows he likes her and will take her to the dance. Everyone knows it."

Katie crossed her arms over her chest and stared at Tennison. She wanted to go to the dance in the worst way possible, but she wanted to go with Ryan and not Peter. *But what if Ryan didn't ask her out and asked Sarah instead? And what if no one else asked her out? What would she do then? That thought was almost unbearable. What if her mother didn't allow her to go because of what she had done today?* All these questions tumbled around in her head like the spin cycle in a washing machine.

"Okay," said Katie, "I'll go with Peter on one condition."

"Anything, you name it, anything," said Tennison with delight.

"That your brother comes and asks me himself."

"It's a deal," squealed Tennison. She grabbed Katie around the waist and spun her around in a circle. "I'll go get him right now." Tennison giggled as she went to the front door. "Katie, I owe you. Thank you. Thank you so much." She slipped out the door and disappeared.

Katie stood in the middle of the living room, not sure what had just happened. *Did I just agree to go to the dance with Tennison's older brother? I haven't met him yet and said yes to attending the biggest dance of the year with someone I don't know. What was I thinking? Why is my life so complicated? Why couldn't it be simple? Why couldn't I go to the dance with someone I liked? What if Peter was the ugliest boy in school? All the other classmates would tease me, and no good-looking boys would ever ask me out again. What if Mom says I couldn't go? That would be as bad as going to the dance with an ugly guy. What will I do?* Her thoughts were interrupted by a knock on the door.

"Ms. Katie, do you want me to get the door?" called Mrs. Sanchez from the kitchen.

"No, I'll get it." She walked to the door and opened it slowly. There, in the hallway, stood a tall, muscular-looking boy. "Can I help you?"

"Katie Sparrow. I'm Peter," the young man said in a quiet but friendly voice. "Can I come in?"

Katie stood there staring at the figure in the hallway. The boy before her wasn't ugly, but he wasn't exactly handsome either. He was cute in an athletic, sporty kind of way. He wasn't as handsome as Ryan, but few boys were that attractive. She looked him over carefully. He had short brown hair and eyes the color of a hazelnut. His nose was thin and slightly pointed but perfectly accented his heart-shaped lips. He wore khaki shorts, old running shoes, and an old gray T-shirt with a hole in the left sleeve. Yes, she decided, he was okay. The best description for him was okay. She liked him.

"Can I come in?" he asked again.

"Why, yes. Please come in," stammered Katie as she tried to wipe the look of surprise off her face. He was more than she had expected. "Have a seat on the couch."

"Who is it?" called Katie's mother from her study.

"Uh, it's only Peter, Mom."

"Peter, who?"

"Just plain Peter," replied Katie.

"What does he want?"

Katie turned to Peter and asked, "What do you want?"

"Katie Sparrow, I want to ask you to go with me to the back-to-school dance at the end of the month."

"He wants to ask me to a dance!" called Katie to her mother.

"Tell him no," said her mother. "We don't know him."

"He's Tennison's brother," said Katie.

"We still don't know him. Tell him no."

"I'll handle it, Mom, okay." She turned back toward Peter and again asked him to sit on the couch. He went to the far corner of the room and sat gently on the edge of the couch.

"Your mom sounds mean," he whispered.

"Only when she's around me," said Katie with a smile. She went to the overstuffed chair and sat. This time, she sat properly with her hands on her knees and back straight, just as she had been taught.

"Who's the boy?" asked Mikey as he entered the room from the kitchen. "Is he your boyfriend? Did you kiss?"

"That's none of your business, Mikey. Now scram before I use you to mop the kitchen floor."

"You don't scare me," said Mikey.

"She scares me," said Peter with a shy grin. Katie smiled back at him and laughed. She liked his sense of humor.

"I'm going to watch television," said Mikey.

"Go in your room to watch television," ordered Katie.

"You're not my mom."

"Mikey, I'll give you a dollar if you go to your room."

"Promise?"

"I promise."

"Okay then." Mikey ran in the direction he had come, and Katie heard his bedroom door slam behind him.

"Now, what did you say?" Katie asked Peter.

"I would like to ask you to the dance. You know, the big dance at Navy Pier."

"I know about the big dance," said Katie. "It's all I've heard about since moving here."

"Well," coughed Peter, "I'd like to take you to the dance."

"But your sister said you didn't want to go."

"That's right, I don't like school dances much. I'd rather play video games, read, or draw, but when she said you might be interested in going to the dance with me, I thought I would give it a whirl."

"A whirl?"

"Yes, I thought I would try it," continued Peter. "I saw you shopping with your nanny, and I thought you looked interesting."

"Interesting?"

"Yes, you looked pretty, smart, and down to earth, unlike my sister's other friends—Sarah, in particular. She really is stuck on herself—a real pain. If you were willing to go with me, I would go to the dance. I know I'm not good-looking, so I'll understand if you rebuff my request. I'm not good at this because I've never asked a girl out before. If I'm making a fool of myself, please tell me."

Katie liked his honesty and how he said things like "whirl," "rebuff," "interesting," and "in particular." She hadn't heard people her age use words like that before. She thought those words were reserved for grown-ups. They were the kind of words her father had used.

"Peter, it's nice of you to ask me to the dance. I'm flattered. I will go to the dance with you if my mother lets me go. Right now, I'm in her doghouse. I've done some silly things recently that she hasn't liked, so she may not let me go."

"Do you want me to ask her for you?"

"No, Peter, I will have to face this alone. I don't think you can help me with this problem."

"Okay." He stood and walked to the door. "I sure hope your mother allows you to go to the dance."

"Me too," said Katie. "Me too," she repeated as she opened the door, and he stepped out into the corridor. "I'll let you know tomorrow."

"That'll work. See you tomorrow."

They shook hands, and he headed toward the elevator. She watched him until the elevator doors closed behind him. He seemed like a nice boy, she thought, the kind of boy you want as your best friend but not the kind you want to date. He was the kind of guy you want to help with your homework and study for a test, but not the kind you want to hold hands with as you walk down the hallway at school. He was okay. Yes, *okay* was exactly the right word to describe Peter. He could never match up to Ryan, which was for sure.

She closed the door and walked to her mother's study. She knocked, and when her mother answered, she stepped inside. "Mom, I've been asked to the big dance by Tennison's brother, Peter. Can I go?"

"Katie, I don't want to talk about it right now. I'm still upset at you for what you did today. Can we talk about the dance tomorrow after I've had a chance to calm down?"

"But I told him I would give him an answer tomorrow."

"I don't care what you told him. I don't want to discuss this right now."

"But I promised," pleaded Katie.

"Okay, you can go, but I want to know all the details. I want to talk to his mother and reserve the right to say no later."

"Okay, thank you, Mom," said Katie. "Also, am I grounded for leaving the house today?"

"You should be, but I will give you another chance. You must promise never to leave the house again without telling Mrs. Sanchez or me where you're going. And I never want you to go to Michigan Avenue by yourself again. Is that understood, young lady?"

"Yes," said Katie.

"Good."

"Mom, you never asked to see the new clothes I bought today. Don't you want to see them?"

"I don't have time right now. How about tomorrow?"

Katie left her mother's study and headed back to her room. Mrs. Sanchez stuck her head out of the kitchen and said, "Ms. Katie, I saw some packages in your room. Did you buy some new clothes? Can I see them?"

"Yes, you can," said Katie. "I would love to show them to you."

They went to her bedroom, and Katie spent the next hour modeling her new clothes for Mrs. Sanchez. She liked how Mrs. Sanchez commented on each new piece and complimented her on the way she looked. When they had finished, Katie sat on the bed next to

Mr. Sanchez. Mrs. Sanchez put her arm around Katie's shoulder and hugged her.

"You look so grown-up in your new clothes," said Mrs. Sanchez. "You're a very beautiful young lady, Ms. Katie."

"Do you think so?"

"Oh yes, I'm very, very sure. You'll be a beautiful woman when you grow up, just like your mother."

"Thank you," whispered Katie. She put her head on Mrs. Sanchez's shoulder and began to cry.

❂

CHAPTER 9

Mrs. Sanchez entered Katie's room at ten o'clock on Sunday morning. Katie had been awake for an hour and was propped up in bed, reading a book. "Ms. Katie, Ms. Tennison is here to see you."

"Please tell her I will be right out." Katie hurriedly slipped on a pair of her new jeans and one of her new tops, which she had washed and ironed last night. She quickly brushed her hair and went out to the living room where Tennison was waiting. "Tennison," said Katie.

"Good morning, Katie. How are you this morning? My brother said you promised to go to the dance with him. I want to thank you. Not only did you save me from utter humiliation, but I want you to know that he's the happiest and most excited I've seen him my whole life. You made his day."

"I did?"

"You sure did. You would think he was going to the dance with Taylor Swift or something. I also stopped by to see if you wanted to go to Navy Pier with a group of us this morning. We usually have breakfast at the pier on Sunday mornings. It's our little ritual. Peter will be there."

"Sure, I'd like that very much."

"See you in the lobby in an hour. And don't forget some money."

"Okay," said Katie.

Tennison left, and Katie got her mother's permission to go. She took a shower and spent an extra few minutes styling her hair. She wanted to look exactly right. She was happy to have new clothes to wear. She looked in the mirror and was pleased with her reflection. *The group would have to accept me now*, she thought.

She kissed her mother and Mrs. Sanchez goodbye. "Be home by three o'clock," her mother called as she entered the hallway.

"Okay, Mom."

A group of teens was already standing in the sitting area when she reached the lobby. She saw Tennison, Peter, Sarah, Ryan, and two other people she didn't know. One was a boy with red hair, and the other was a girl with pale skin and pink hair.

"When she approached the group, Sarah looked at her and said, "Well, if it isn't Country Kathy."

"My name is Katie."

"Oh yes, I remember, Country Katie."

"No, it's just plain Katie."

"Yes, I agree. You are only 'Plain Katie.'"

Katie scowled at Sarah in disgust. "Whatever you say, Sarah."

"Now, now," said Tennison. "Let's try to be friends. Katie, you look cute. Are those new clothes?"

"Yes, I bought them yesterday." Katie looked at Ryan and smiled at him as if to let him know she wouldn't share their secret with Sarah. He smiled back and winked.

"As they say, 'You can take the girl out of the country, but you can't take the country out of the girl,'" said Sarah with a smirk.

"Let's be nice," said Tennison.

"I think you look pretty," said Peter in a low, soft voice.

"Thank you, Peter," replied Katie.

"This is Rebecca," continued Tennison, pointing at the pale girl with pink hair. "And this handsome guy is Ted."

"I am pleased to meet you both," said Katie.

"Let's get started," said Tennison. "Tyler, Rome, and Stevie will meet us there."

The group left the building and walked down Illinois Avenue toward Navy Pier. As they walked, Peter moved close to Katie. "Did you ask your mom about the dance?"

"Yes, she said maybe."

"That's great. I'm really looking forward to it," he said with a grin.

"So am I," Katie lied. Seeing Ryan this morning convinced her that she would rather go with him to the dance than Peter. Peter was okay, but he wasn't Ryan. She glanced in Ryan's direction and wished it were her hand he held instead of Sarah's.

They hooked up with Tyler, Rome, and Stevie when they reached Navy Pier. They went into the mall area. There was a group of acrobats on the center stage doing juggling tricks. They were very good, so the group stopped and watched for a few minutes. One of the jugglers left the stage looking for a volunteer from the crowd to assist him with the act. He first looked at Tennison and then at Katie. Katie grabbed Peter's arm and hid behind him. She was too embarrassed and didn't want to get on stage before all these people.

Sarah jumped up and down and waved her arms. She wanted the juggler to pick her. She grabbed the juggler's hand, and he reluctantly took her on the stage with him. She stood on the corner of the stage and danced and clapped her hands to the music playing on the sound system. She seemed to enjoy herself. She was a natural showoff.

Katie smiled as Sarah performed with the jugglers. *She must not know how ridiculous she looks*, thought Katie.

One of the jugglers grabbed Sarah's hand and moved her to the center of the stage. He then made her hold her hands out in front of her and asked her to point her index fingers toward the audience. He took a tin pie plate and began to spin it on his index finger. Once it was spinning very fast, he placed it on Sarah's finger. He then started another plate and put it on her other finger. He kept hitting the pie plates with the palms of his hands to keep them moving. Satisfied that both plates would keep spinning, he grabbed a plastic rose from a nearby table and placed it in Sarah's mouth. She looked silly. Everyone in the audience laughed.

The juggler reached under the table, took out an old red wig, and placed it on Sarah's head. The bangs on the wig covered her eyes. She looked like a Raggedy Ann doll. Katie couldn't help herself; she laughed so hard she had to hold her sides.

She was enjoying Sarah's humiliation when she felt someone touch her elbow. She turned around. It was Ryan. He motioned for her to join him at the back of the crowd. She let go of Peter's arm. He was so engrossed in the juggling act that he didn't notice as she slipped away and carefully worked her way to the back of the room with Ryan.

"What is it?" asked Katie. She almost had to shout because the music on the stage was so loud.

"I wanted you to know I had a great time shopping with you yesterday," he shouted.

She leaned toward him and yelled, "I had a nice time too. I am so sorry about my mother."

"That's okay. That stuff happens." He smiled. "I understand."

"I can't believe how comfortable I feel around you," said Katie. "I thought I would be nervous to see you again after yesterday's fiasco."

"I'm glad," shouted Ryan.

"Me too."

"Since we had such a good time yesterday, I thought you might want to go to the big dance with me at the end of the month. What do you think?"

Katie couldn't believe her ears. *Had Ryan just asked me to the back-to-school dance?* "What did you say?" she asked with a puzzled look.

"I asked you to the dance," he shouted.

"That's what I thought you said."

"Well?"

"Yes," she screamed, but she screamed her answer just as the music stopped, and her yell echoed through the building—yes… yes…yes…yes. Katie's face turned red with embarrassment. She looked up on stage and saw Sarah staring at her. Her eyes were wild with anger. She had a crazed look about her. Katie looked around the room and realized everyone in the building was staring at her too. Then they turned back toward the stage and started to clap for Sarah's part in the juggling act.

Katie looked back at Ryan. He smiled and said, "I'm glad you're going to the dance with me."

"Me too," she said. "I guess you had better go rescue Sarah from her fans."

"Yes, I better go." He smiled at her again and reached out and touched her hand. He then moved through the crowd toward the stage. Katie stood there, frozen in place, and realized how foolish she was. *How would I go to the dance with Ryan when I have already told Peter I would go with him? How would I tell Peter I couldn't go to the dance with him after he had been so nice to ask me first?* He was such a nice guy, and she didn't want to hurt his feelings. *And what would Sarah do to me once she learns that Ryan had asked me to the dance?*

Suddenly, Katie felt sick to her stomach, like she would throw up on the crowd in front of her. She took a deep breath and put her hands on her stomach. When her head cleared and her stomach settled, she returned to Peter.

"Hey, Katie," said Peter, "where have you been? I've been looking for you."

"I wanted to get out of the crowd for a second," she lied. I needed to get some fresh air. "My stomach was bothering me."

"Let's ride the Ferris wheel before we eat breakfast," said Peter.

"That sounds like fun," said Katie hesitantly. She wasn't sure her stomach could take the excitement of riding the ten-story tall Ferris wheel, but she was willing to try.

Katie and Peter walked with the others to the upper deck of Navy Pier where the mammoth Ferris wheel stood. It looked like it touched the sky.

"I'll get the tickets," said Peter. He hurried off with Ryan and Tyler toward the barn-red ticket shack that stood on the other side of the miniature golf course. Katie watched as they disappeared.

"What were you and Ryan talking about?" asked Sarah. "I told you, country girl, to leave Ryan alone. Don't you hear well? Do you know what 'leave alone' means? You're the dumbest country girl I've ever met."

Katie stood there and glared at Sarah. She couldn't believe how mean one girl could be to another. Girls in Alpine had never acted this way. And she knew Camden would never have talked to her in such a tone of voice. She wanted to cry, but she wasn't going to give Sarah the satisfaction of thinking she had hurt her feelings. She fought hard to keep her emotions in check so the tears wouldn't flow down her cheeks.

"Don't talk to Katie like that," said Tennison.

"You stay out of this, Tennison. This is between me and the country girl."

"Her name is Katie."

"No, it's not," continued Sarah. "Her name is now mud. She knows better than to flirt with someone else's boyfriend. Why did she come with us anyway?"

"Because my brother, Peter, asked her to come."

"What does a good-looking guy like your brother see in this mousy country girl anyway? Or did he ask her to come because he felt sorry for her? I'm sure that's it. He felt sorry for poor, old Country Katie."

"We've got the tickets," the boys yelled in unison as they approached the group.

"Since the cars only hold four at a time," said Peter, "we decided to break the group up. We're going to go in twos. To make it fair, I'm going to write each girl's name on a slip of paper and put them in my baseball hat. Then, each boy will pull a piece of paper from the hat. The girl whose name is called will go on the ride with that boy. Understood?"

"That's a crazy idea," said Sarah. "I'm going on the ride with Ryan."

"No," said Peter. "Everyone has agreed to do it this way. You're outnumbered."

Peter quickly tore up some paper he had gotten from the ticket counter and wrote each girl's name on a piece, folded it, and put it in his Chicago Cubs hat. He held the hat over his head. "Okay, Ted, you're first."

Ted reached into the hat and pulled out the first slip of paper. Ted looked at it and said," Stevie, you're with me."

Stevie and Ted walked toward the entrance to the Ferris wheel. Next, Tyler reached into the hat and pulled out Rebecca's name. They, too, went to the Ferris wheel. It was now Ryan's turn. He reached into the hat and pulled out a slip of paper. He held it up and said, "Katie, it looks like you're with me."

"That can't be," shouted Sarah. "Let me see that piece of paper." She grabbed the small piece of paper from Ryan's hand and examined it carefully. She threw the paper on the ground and stomped on it. "I don't care what that piece of paper says. Ryan is going on the Ferris wheel with me, and that's final."

"Come on, Sarah. The rules are the rules," sighed Ryan.

"I'm not going to allow you to go on the ride with that ugly little country girl," said Sarah.

Katie stood there and looked at her shoes. She didn't want to see the scene between Sarah and Ryan that was playing out. It embarrassed her.

"Sarah, I'm riding with Katie," said Ryan. "Let's go, Katie."

Katie moved toward Ryan, but Sarah jumped in front of her. "You better think this over, country girl. If you want to have any friends at all, you'd better stop where you are and let me go on the ride with Ryan."

Ryan moved Sarah aside and grabbed Katie's hand. He pulled Katie toward the platform for the ride. Katie wanted to go with Ryan in the worst way. She wanted nothing more than to spend a few minutes alone with him, but she stopped and looked into his eyes. "I don't want to cause any trouble," she said. "I think you had better go with Sarah."

"But I want to go on the ride with you."

"We'll do it some other time," said Katie. She pulled her hand out of Ryan's and walked back to Peter.

"You're smarter than I gave you credit for, country girl," said Sarah as she grabbed Ryan's hand. "Let's go, Ryan, and leave that loser alone."

Reluctantly, Ryan followed Sarah to the platform. He looked back over his shoulder at Katie. Katie's heart sank from her chest to her toes. She wished she were walking to the platform with Ryan but knew it was best to let Sarah have her way. It was better to lose one battle than to lose the entire war.

"Well, it looks like you're stuck with me," said Peter.

"I'm glad I'm going on the ride with you," Katie lied. Silently, she walked to the Ferris wheel with Peter. They waited their turn to enter one of the big, red, enclosed cars that made up the ride.

Once they were inside and seated on opposite benches, Peter looked at Katie and said, "I know you like Ryan. It's obvious how you look at him when he's around you. That's okay with me. I still would like to take you to the dance."

"Can we talk about the dance?" asked Katie.

"Sure, what's on your mind?"

The big Ferris wheel suddenly jerked, causing the car they were riding in to swing back and forth awkwardly. It scared Katie. She'd never been in a Ferris wheel this large, and the car's swaying at this height made her feel like she would fall. She screamed.

Peter jumped off his bench and quickly sat down beside her. "We're going to be all right," he assured her. "This type of thing happens all the time. This Ferris wheel is very sturdy and strong. It won't fall, I promise. I'll sit right here with you, so you won't be frightened."

"Thank you, Peter. I'm normally much braver than this on rides. The sudden jerk startled me, that's all." For some reason, she felt safer with Peter by her side. He was so kind and thoughtful. She looked into his eyes, and there was a gentleness there, a sense of kindness she hadn't seen in anyone's eyes since her father had passed away. She realized that Peter had her father's eyes: soft, gentle, almost melancholy.

"I understand. Now, what did you want to tell me about the dance?" asked Peter.

For some reason, she had lost the desire to talk about it. He was so kind; how could she ever get up the nerve to tell him she didn't want to go to the dance with him and that she wanted to go with Ryan? She didn't want to hurt his feelings. "Nothing. I don't want to talk about the dance right now. We can discuss it later when we're on the ground."

"Sure, whatever you say," said Peter.

They remained silent the rest of the ride. Katie looked out the window at Lake Michigan and watched the sailboats dancing along its glassy surface with their bright white sails billowing in the gentle breeze. She also looked north toward Lincoln Park and marveled at the tall condo buildings that lined the shore of the lake.

By the time they reached the ground, the rest of the group was waiting for them by the miniature golf course. "What took you two so long?" asked Tennison.

"We had a problem with our car," answered Peter.

Katie looked up at Peter and smiled. "Thank you, Peter, for covering for me. I appreciate that you didn't tell them I screamed."

"You're welcome." He grinned. They walked slowly toward the group. "Now we're on the ground, what did you want to tell me about the dance?"

CHAPTER 10

Katie tried hard for the next few days to avoid Ryan, Sarah, Tennison, and Peter. She hadn't had the courage to tell Peter she didn't want to go to the dance with him while they were at Navy Pier, and she didn't dare tell Ryan she hadn't told Peter. It was a circle without an end, a problem without a solution, and an issue without a clear path to resolution. None of her options seemed reasonable.

She spent her days helping Mrs. Sanchez around the condo with the final boxes that needed to be unpacked. She liked Mrs. Sanchez's warm, toothy grin and funny stories. She started to learn a little Spanish as they talked while they worked. Katie's Spanish was crude, but Mrs. Sanchez pretended to understand.

As they busied themselves with the housework, they turned the radio to a Spanish-speaking station and sang the songs together. Katie wasn't sure what she was singing, but she belted out each chorus with energy and gusto. When the song ended, they'd burst out laughing until tears ran down their cheeks. Mrs. Sanchez would grab Katie by the arm and say, "Ms. Katie, I'm going to make you a Mexican señorita yet."

Doing the housework with Mrs. Sanchez was fun and made her forget her problems with Peter and Ryan for a few minutes. As she and Mrs. Sanchez cleaned, danced, sang, and laughed around the house, Katie wished she and her mother could have this much fun together; but her mother worked later and later each day and never seemed to be around.

Mikey had found some new friends in the building and spent more of his time away from home on play dates. Mikey was enjoying himself and was back to his pesky self again. He hadn't mentioned Utah or his friends in Alpine for several days. Katie was surprised at how quickly he had adapted to city life in Chicago while her heart was deeply entrenched in the tree-lined streets of Alpine.

As the days passed, Katie found herself thinking more about Camden. She wished that Camden could visit Chicago for a couple of weeks before school started, but she knew she couldn't because her parents were taking her to San Diego for summer vacation. She missed her friend very much. She wanted to discuss her problem with Ryan and Peter and get Camden's advice.

"What are you thinking about?" asked Mrs. Sanchez. "You look miles away."

"Nothing," sighed Katie. She slumped down on the couch in the living room and propped one of the gray throw pillows behind her head.

"I think someone is homesick," said Mrs. Sanchez. "I remember when I left Mexico to come to America. It took me almost three months to stop crying. Every time I would think of home, I'd burst into tears. Even now, after all these years, I will cry as I remember growing up. It's silly, really. I couldn't wait to get out of Mexico when I lived there. There was so much poverty, crime, and dirt. Everything was gritty with dust. I never felt clean when I was there, but it was home, and now that I'm older, I miss it very much.

"I don't think I'm homesick," Katie lied. "I think I'm just tired from the move and have a headache."

"You should put on your pajamas and jump into bed. I can finish cleaning up."

"I think I will." Katie's head pounded, and her body ached. Her brain felt too big for her skull, and it felt like it was trying to get out of her head. She leaned over and kissed Mrs. Sanchez on the cheek. "Mrs. Sanchez, you're my best friend here in Chicago."

"Thank you, Ms. Katie," said Mrs. Sanchez with a grin.

Katie walked slowly to her bedroom and put on her pajamas. She climbed into her bed and tightly pulled the covers under her chin.

"Here are two aspirins and a glass of water," said Mrs. Sanchez.

"Thank you. I'm going to try to sleep."

Katie didn't know how long she had slept but woke up to her mother sitting on the side of her bed with a worried look on her face. Katie felt terrible.

"Katie, how do you feel?" asked her mother.

"Not very good."

"You're burning up. Your temperature is close to 104 degrees."

"How can that be?" said Katie. "I feel like I'm freezing to death." She pulled the blanket up tighter to her chin.

"Fevers do funny things to our bodies," said her mother. "I don't like this high temperature at all. I'm worried. We need to take you to the doctor right now."

"I don't want to go to the doctor. Let me sleep. I'll be better in the morning."

"No, that won't do. Fever isn't something you mess with. A fever is a sign that your body gives to tell us something is seriously wrong. Wrap this blanket around you and put on your slippers. I'll meet you in the living room in a few minutes after I call the doctor." Katie's mother got off the bed and out of the room.

Katie sat in bed and looked around. It was dark outside. She looked at the clock on her nightstand. It was midnight. She tried to stand, but her head felt like a two-ton wrecking ball, and it hurt her to lift it. She was terribly dizzy; her brain spun in her head like the rinse cycle of a washing machine. She lay back on the bed and closed her eyes.

"Katie, get up," shouted her mother through the bedroom doorway.

"I can't. My head really hurts."

"Try."

"I did try, but I got very dizzy."

"Did you really try?"

"Yes, Mom, I really tried," said Katie. Her head continued to pound, and now she felt like she would throw up.

"Okay, I'll call Dr. Williams and see if he'll make a house call as a favor to me. His clinic is next to my office. You know it would be easier if you let me take you to the hospital."

"Sorry, Mom, but I can't get up."

"You don't take care of yourself. You're always running around the house without socks on your feet. I think you like being sick and making me worry."

"I didn't want to get sick," said Katie weakly. She had to force herself to keep from throwing up.

Why does Mom always think everything is my fault? Ever since Dad died, Mom thinks everything that goes wrong is my fault. I wish Daddy were here to take care of me.

Her mother left the room to call Dr. Williams. Katie closed her eyes and fell into a fitful sleep.

Katie woke to a cold, clammy hand on her forehead. She looked up through bloodshot, fiery eyes and saw a gray-haired man looking down at her. The strange face frightened her.

"Hi, Katie, I'm Dr. Williams," said the man. He was a large man with a round, red, blotchy face and oversized cheeks that were the size of grapefruits. Because of the size of his cheeks, his eyes were mere slits. "You're a very sick young lady."

Why do old people always use the term "young lady" when they talk to teenagers? She hated it when people called her that. Couldn't he see she was just a teenage girl, not a young lady?

Dr. Williams put the back of his cold, chubby hand on her forehead and then picked up her hand by the wrist. He put his finger on her pulse, looked at his watch, and counted her heartbeats.

Katie's mother stepped from behind the doctor. "Katie, dear, how do you feel?"

"Not good."

"I think she might have a case of mononucleosis," said Dr. Williams.

"She couldn't have mono," said Mom. "How and where would she have gotten mono? Mono is known as the kissing disease, and my daughter hasn't kissed anyone."

"Dr. Sparrow," said Dr. Williams, "I'm sure you know mononucleosis can be transmitted in other ways than kissing. It can spread when people share the same eating utensils—knives, forks, and spoons. It can also be transferred if people share the same drinking straw. The mononucleosis virus spreads through the saliva. Has your daughter eaten from other people's eating utensils or shared a drinking straw with anyone?

Katie's mother looked at her and asked, "Katie, did you share a drinking straw with someone or eat off their fork?"

Katie thought for a moment. The only person she remembered sharing silverware with was when she ate a slice of cake with Camden just before she moved to Chicago. "I shared a fork with Camden."

"Had Camden been sick when you ate from her fork?" asked Dr. Williams. He shifted his massive weight on the bed, and it caused Katie to slide toward him. She had to scoot back to the middle of the bed to avoid bumping into him.

"I don't think so," said Katie.

"The only other thing it could be is stress and anxiety. Stress and anxiety, when they reach their peak, can give you the same symptoms as you're exhibiting. Have you been under any stress lately?" asked Dr. Williams.

"Yes," said Katie's mother. "We just moved to Chicago from Utah, and Katie's father passed away about six months ago."

"Well, that certainly could cause these symptoms. It is either mononucleosis or stress. If it's mono, then I'm afraid she won't be going anywhere for the next three to four weeks, but if it's stress-related, we can have her back on her feet in just a few days—maybe a week."

"Three or four weeks?" said Katie. "I have a very important dance I must attend in three weeks. I can't miss the dance."

"I'm sorry, young lady, but you won't be going to any dance if you have mono."

There was that phrase again, but this time, it didn't bother her as badly as the news she might not be able to attend the dance. The news was terrible. *How could this be happening to me?* she wondered. *Why is my life so miserable?*

"I must go to the dance," she whispered. "I just have to."

"Stick out your tongue," said Dr. Williams. "I need to get a sample of your saliva on this cotton swab to send to the lab for testing. That's the only way we'll know what you have and how to treat you properly." He moved the cotton swab circularly inside Katie's mouth and throat. He then slipped the swab into a clean test tube, sealed it with a small cork, took a black marker, and wrote Katie's name and the date on the tube.

"I want you to take these pills," said Dr. Williams as he handed Katie two tiny blue pills and the glass of water that sat on the nightstand. "They will help you sleep and hopefully cause your fever to come down. I'll call you tomorrow to let you know the test results."

Dr. Williams hoisted his bulk off Katie's bed. He bent over and slipped the test tube into his leather bag. Katie's mom escorted him to the door.

"Sleep well, young lady," said Dr. Williams as he maneuvered his massive frame through the doorway.

Katie knew she wouldn't sleep. She was too worried about the dance. She was so worried and upset about the possibility of being unable to attend the dance that Dr. Williams's comment about "young lady" didn't even faze her. *What am I going to do about Peter and Ryan?* she wondered.

❧

CHAPTER 11

Katie tossed and turned all night. Between the fever and worrying about the dance, she only slept for a few minutes. And when she did drift off to sleep, her dreams switched between Peter and Ryan. She dreamed about how disappointed Peter would be when she finally dared to tell him she couldn't go to the dance with him and how happy she would be to spend the evening dancing with Ryan.

Peter was a nice boy, and she hated hurting his feelings. He had been kind to her and was among the first to make her feel welcome in Chicago. But Ryan was so handsome, cool, and suave; she couldn't picture herself going to the dance with anyone else.

In the morning, Katie's mom entered the bedroom and put her hand on Katie's forehead. "It feels like your temperature is down a little," she said. "That's a good sign."

Katie tried to force a smile, but even her mouth ached. "When will Dr. Williams call with the test results?"

"I'm not sure," said Mom. "It will be sometime in the early afternoon. The labs are processing the saliva cultures, and it takes time to total all the test results."

"You know I have to go the dance, don't you, Mom?"

"Don't worry about that now. You need to concentrate on getting better, and then we can talk about the dance."

"Okay," said Katie.

"I've asked Mrs. Sanchez to come in early today to care for you. She should be here any minute."

"What?" stammered Katie. "Aren't you staying home with me today?"

"I'm sorry, sweetie, but I have a complicated root canal to perform for a very important patient."

"You mean I'm not as important as your patients?"

"You know you're important to me, but I must make a living to help pay for everything you and Mikey have. Money doesn't grow on trees, you know. Now that your dad is gone, someone must bring home a paycheck. Be a big girl and give me some support."

Katie didn't say another word. She rolled on her side and pulled the pillow over her head. *How could she leave me when I'm sick*, she wondered. *She doesn't love me. What have I done to make her dislike me so much? She would stay home if it were Mikey who was sick.* She felt tears seep onto the pillowcase. All she wanted was to be as close to her mother again as she had been before her father died. She wanted things to return to how they had been when they were a happy family in Alpine, Utah.

Katie heard the door to her room shut. She rolled on her back and looked up at the ceiling. She felt alone and unloved. The realization that no one cared about her hurt her badly. She stared at the ceiling until her eyes became heavy and went to sleep.

"Ms. Katie?" whispered Mrs. Sanchez. "Are you awake?"

Katie opened her eyes and stared up into Mrs. Sanchez's smiling face.

"It's time to take the pills that Dr. Williams left for you."

"What time is it?" asked Katie. She swallowed two more of the blue pills and took a sip of water.

"It's noon. You were sleeping so soundly I didn't want to wake you."

"Has my mother called?"

"No," sighed Mrs. Sanchez. "Are you hungry?"

"She hasn't called to check up on me?" asked Katie.

Mrs. Sanchez shook her head. "No, she hasn't. I'm sorry." There was an awkward silence as Katie and Mrs. Sanchez stared at each other. "I'm sure she is terribly busy and thinking about you right now."

Katie looked at her disappointedly.

"I've made some homemade chicken noodle soup for you. Would you like a bowl?" said Mrs. Sanchez.

"Yes," said Katie.

"And someone outside your door wants to see you." Mrs. Sanchez walked to the door and opened it. There in the hallway stood Mikey.

He stepped inside the doorway. "How are you feeling?" he squeaked, unsure what to say.

"Okay," replied Katie.

"I hope you get better soon. I'm worried about you. Mom told me I can't go into your room because I might catch whatever you've got, so I must stay by the doorway. I sure wish I could hug you."

"I'm glad someone is worried about me," said Katie, "because Mom isn't."

"I'm worried about you too," said Mrs. Sanchez with her warm smile.

"A boy named Peter stopped by this morning," continued Mikey.

"He did? What did he say?"

"He wanted to talk to you. He said he hadn't seen you in a few days and wondered if you were okay."

"What did you tell him?" asked Katie.

"I told him you were sick. What was I supposed to tell him?"

Katie sighed. "You did the right thing, Mikey. You're a good brother. Did anyone else call or come to the door while I was asleep? Did Ryan call or come by?"

"No one by that name," said Mikey.

Suddenly, the ringing of the telephone interrupted their conversation. "I'll get it," said Mrs. Sanchez. "You two can continue to talk." She left the room and answered the phone in the kitchen.

"Mikey, why doesn't Mom like me?" asked Katie.

"She does."

"She doesn't show it. She treats me like I've got leprosy or something, as if she would catch a disease if she got too close to me."

Mikey squatted down in the doorway. "It might be that you look so much like Dad. You know you have his smile and his eyes. It might be hard for Mom to see so much of Dad in you. Looking at you might bring back memories."

Katie turned on her side to get a better look at Mikey. "You might be right. I'd never thought of that before. You're a smart boy, Mikey, for only seven years old."

"Hey, I'm almost eight years old. I'm not a little kid anymore."

"I know that. I wish I could give you a big hug right now."

"Yuck," groaned Mikey with a smile.

Mrs. Sanchez walked back into the room with a gigantic grin. "That was your mother on the phone. She said she just spoke to Dr. Williams, and the test results came back negative."

"What does that mean?" asked Katie with a puzzled look. "What does negative mean? Is it something bad?"

"No, it means you don't have mono. Dr. Williams said you have a stress-related illness that's not contagious. He told your mom you should be as good as new in a few days. You need to rest."

"Yippee!" screamed Mikey as he ran to Katie's bed, threw his arms around her neck, and kissed her on the cheek.

"I thought you said hugs and kisses were yucky?"

"Not when you've found out your big sister is going to be okay."

"I'm starting to feel better already. Mrs. Sanchez, I'm ready for your chicken noodle soup."

For the next few hours, Katie slept. She forgot about her problems and dreamed of Alpine and Camden. She dreamed about the hikes they had taken through the mountains that surrounded Alpine and the feel of the clean, cold water on her skin as they waded through the streams. She dreamed of the games they played with the other neighborhood kids: kick-the-can, hide-and-seek, tag, and kickball. In her dreams, she was happy and safe.

In one of her dreams, she was with her dad, throwing the ball around with him and Mikey. Her dad looked so handsome and strong.

Katie woke to a knock on her bedroom door. Mrs. Sanchez was standing in the doorway. "Do you feel well enough for guests? If you are, there is a boy here to see you. Should I let him in?"

"Who is it? Is it Ryan?"

"He says his name is Peter. He's very handsome," said Mrs. Sanchez with a wink.

"Give me a minute and let me put on a robe and brush my hair."

Mrs. Sanchez smiled and walked out of the room. Katie got out of bed, put on her bathrobe, grabbed her brush off the night-stand, and frantically brushed the knots and tangles from her hair. She thought, *This would be a good time to tell him I can't go to the dance with him. If I get it over with right now, it will be one less problem I'll have to think about. Yes, that is the best thing to do: just tell him the truth and be done with it.* Katie put the brush back on the nightstand and propped herself in bed just as the door opened.

Peter tiptoed into the room as if poisonous snakes were coiled up and covering the floor. He smiled at Katie. "How are you feeling?" he whispered.

"Much better since you're here." She pointed at a chair in the corner. "Throw those clothes on the floor and sit."

Peter went to the wicker chair with its high back and pink cushions and removed Katie's orange sweatshirt and dark-blue socks. He sat on the edge, frightened he would break the chair if he put his entire weight on it. He looked like a tall, slender bird teetering on a perch. It made her smile.

"Your mom says you've got some kind of stress-related illness. She says you should be up and around in a few days."

"You talked to my mom?" asked Katie.

"I sure did. I had to ask her a question."

"You actually talked to my mom?"

"Yes, about two hours ago."

"Why did you call my mom?" asked Katie.

"I'll tell you later. Right now, I want to know how you're feeling?"

"To tell you the truth, my head is still sore, and my back aches. But I feel much better than I did last night."

"That's good."

"Have you seen Ryan or Sarah lately?" asked Katie calmly and uninterestedly. She didn't want to sound too anxious to find out about Ryan. She absentmindedly wrapped a wisp of her hair around her index finger.

"Yes, Tennison and I were with them on Michigan Avenue yesterday. They seem happy when they're together." Peter slid back a little further on the chair, trying to find a comfortable position.

"What?" said Katie.

"They always seem to have a good time together," continued Peter. "They seem made for each other."

"Oh." The image of Ryan and Sarah having a good time on Michigan Avenue caused Katie's stomach to ache; and she had an odd, strange, tight sensation in her chest. *Is this what jealousy felt like?* she wondered.

"I think they like each other," said Peter.

"That can't be," stammered Katie. "That can't be."

"Why not?"

"I don't know, but it can't be. Ryan doesn't seem to like her much when I'm around."

"Nobody can keep their eyes off you when you're around. Everyone thinks you're the prettiest girl in the neighborhood."

"That's not true." Katie blushed. She wondered if it was true, or if Peter was trying to make her feel better.

"I've got something to tell you," said Peter. He fidgeted nervously in the chair as if ants were crawling on his body. He didn't know what to do with his hands and kept rubbing his legs as if he were giving himself a massage.

"I need to tell you something first," said Katie. She knew she had to tell him now that she couldn't go to the dance with him. If she didn't, she never would. She rearranged the pillows behind her back, took a deep breath, and said, "Peter, I'm sorry, but I can't—"

But before she could finish, Peter interrupted her and said, "No, I must tell you something first. I need to tell you why I called your mother today. I didn't tell you earlier, and I need to get it off my chest." He stood up from the wicker chair and began to pace back and forth in front of the bed.

"What's so important and mysterious?"

"I called your mom because I had to ask her permission."

"Permission for what?" Now, Katie was curious. She wondered what could be so important that Peter would call her mother.

"I had to ask her permission to buy you something."

"Buy me something?"

"Yes, I wanted to see if I could buy you something. And when I told your mother what I wanted to buy you, she permitted me to get it. She wasn't going to permit me initially, but after I talked to her and told her why I wanted to buy it for you, she finally gave in." Peter was so nervous he almost choked on his words. He kept pacing back and forth, and he talked like a man who was sentenced to death, and this was his final hour of life. "I've never bought anything for a girl except my sister Tennison, so I hope you like it. At first, I wasn't sure if I should get it for you, but then I saw it, and at that moment, I knew it was perfect for you and would make you happy."

"Peter, would you please stop pacing around like a long-tail cat in a room full of rocking chairs and show me what it is before I burst?" said Katie enthusiastically. She was excited to see what it was.

"I can take it back if you don't like it."

"Would you please be quiet and let me see it? I'm sure I'll like it."

Peter walked over to the door and went into the hallway. He retrieved a large cardboard box with holes in the lid. Katie thought she heard a whimper. Carefully, he set the box on the bed in Katie's lap. "Go ahead. Open it," he said.

She removed the lid and looked inside. "Oh my."

"Do you like her?" asked Peter.

"I love her!" exclaimed Katie. She reached into the box, took out a black and gray puppy, and set it on her chest. The puppy stuck out its long, pink tongue and licked Katie's chin. "What kind of dog is she?"

"She's a miniature Schnauzer," replied Peter. They're one of the most loving and caring dogs in the world. They're gentle and don't shed hair all over the house like other dogs. That's why your mom let me buy her for you."

"Where did you find such an adorable puppy?"

"My dad has a friend in St. Charles, about one hour west of Chicago, who raises miniature Schnauzers. He owed my dad a favor, so I was able to pick this one out and buy her quite cheaply. Not that the dog is cheap. On the contrary, her parents are both champions."

"She's beautiful. I've always wanted a dog. But my mom never let me get one. In fact, before my father died, he told me he was going to get me a puppy even if my mom said no. You are so thoughtful, Peter. She's exactly what I want and need."

"I'm so glad."

"What's her name?" asked Katie.

"It can be whatever you want it to be. But the man in St. Charles called her Tex."

"Tex? I like that name. I think I'm going to call her Tex."

"Don't you want to give her a more feminine-sounding name like Lucy, Daisy, or Scarlet?" asked Peter.

"Nope. She looks like a Tex to me." Katie squeezed the puppy and let it nuzzle its nose under her chin.

"I think she likes you." Peter grinned. He was pleased with his choice of gifts. "I think she's going to make you feel better quickly."

"I agree." Katie laughed.

"Now, what did you want to tell me?" asked Peter with a pleased but sheepish grin.

Katie gulped.

✄

CHAPTER 12

Katie couldn't believe her mother had allowed Peter to get her such a wonderful gift. Was her mother changing, or was she trying to feel less guilty for how she treated Katie the past few months? Katie wasn't sure but was glad to have a new friend.

That night, when Katie's mother returned home from work and came into her bedroom to check on her, she gathered her courage and asked, "Mom, why did you let me have a puppy?"

"Oh, I don't know. I felt like you needed something to focus on besides new clothes. If you have a dog to take care of, you won't be able to run off shopping on Michigan Avenue alone. Dogs are a big responsibility, especially in a big city like Chicago."

"Thanks, Mom. I really like the puppy and promise to take good care of her."

"You better because if it messes on the floor, it's going to be your fault, and you'll be responsible for cleaning it up. Do you understand? I'm not going to take care of her for you. You're old enough to take care of it by yourself."

"Mom, the puppy's not an 'it,'" said Katie. "She has a name. It's Tex."

"Tex, Mex, Rex, Lex—I don't care what its name is, just make sure it doesn't mess in the house."

Katie watched her mother leave the room. *How can my mother turn a happy time, like getting a puppy, into a sad and dreary thing?* she wondered. *Why does Mom always rain on my parade and try to make me feel bad?*

Dr. Williams had Katie stay in bed for several days. She still got unbelievably bad headaches, but they quickly passed, and it seemed that each hour, she felt a little bit better.

Having Tex around to play with lifted her spirits and made her forget how tired and sick she was. The puppy made her forget about her mother and how she treated her. It was great to have a pet. She'd never had a dog before, and she couldn't believe how quickly she came to love the little fur ball with her vivid pink tongue, cold, wet nose, and warm brown eyes.

Since Katie couldn't get out of bed, she appreciated that Mikey and Mrs. Sanchez took turns taking Tex down the freight elevator to walk the fuzzy bundle outside. She could tell that Mikey liked Tex as much as she did. She could see it in his eyes and how he softly and gently caressed the new addition to the family. He even took over the feeding and watering chores without being asked. *Mikey's growing up*, she thought.

Peter stopped by every afternoon; and they listened to music, read books, talked, or watched a movie on Netflix. He liked the same music as she did, and he read to her from her favorite *Harry Potter* books. Katie liked their time together because he always found a way to make her laugh, and she liked that. She felt comfortable around him, as though they had known each other their entire lives.

"I'm going to be a writer when I graduate from college," said Peter. "I want to write novels like Amor Towles, Ernest Hemingway, and John Steinbeck."

"You already know what you want to be?" asked Katie.

"Yes, I do. I love books, and nothing is better than telling a good story. Before I sleep at night, I think about the stories I will write someday."

"All I want to do is finish high school and college. That's as far as I've thought ahead. All I know is I don't want to be a dentist like my mother because it's made her mean and cranky."

"Do you think being a dentist has made her that way?" asked Peter.

"I don't know if her job made her unhappy, but something has turned her into the Wicked Witch of the West. She doesn't smile anymore. She always smiled when my dad was alive and before she started practicing dentistry again. She was always so happy."

"Maybe it's not her job. Maybe she misses your dad."

"I don't know what it is, but she's changed even more since we moved to Chicago. I love her, but I don't like being around her as much as I used to. And I don't think she likes being around me either."

"That can't be true, Katie, because I like being around you," said Peter. His cheeks turned a bright red, and a faint hint of a smile crept across his thin lips.

Katie smiled back at him and said, "I like the time we spend together too."

Peter's frequent visits to the condo did not stop her from thinking about Ryan. She wondered why he hadn't visited and why he hadn't called. She missed him, and every time she thought of him and his magnificent smile, she got a knot in her stomach.

She still hadn't found the courage to tell Peter she wasn't going to be able to go to the school dance with him, and every day that went by made it harder and harder. She didn't want to hurt his feelings. He had been so nice to her that she didn't want to make him feel bad, but she had to follow her heart. She had to tell him—and soon. *But how was she going to tell him? When would be the right time? And how would he react?*

Before she went to sleep that night, she rehearsed in her mind the words and phrases she would use to tell him: "Peter, I like you as a friend very much. And I appreciate you asking me to the dance, but I don't think I'm the right girl for you. You need to take someone more interesting and fun." Or "Peter, I've thought it over and decided you need to go to the dance with someone else. I'm not pretty or good enough for you." Or "Peter, I appreciate you asking me to the dance, but I can't go with you. I don't have a pretty dress like the other girls, and I don't want to embarrass you." But no matter what words, phrases, or excuses she used, they all sounded lame and weak. They all sounded like a lie, which they were. *Why is it so hard to say no?* she wondered.

The next morning, she had another of her terrible headaches. It felt like someone was inside her head, beating a hammer against her skull.

Mrs. Sanchez stuck her head through the bedroom door and asked how she felt.

"Not so good this morning, Mrs. Sanchez," replied Katie.

"Do you want any breakfast? I can cook you some nice hot oatmeal or scramble you and egg."

"No, I don't want anything to eat. But can I ask you a question and get your advice?"

"Sure, Ms. Katie, you can ask me anything except my age. But if it's personal, shouldn't you ask your mother?"

"No, I can't ask my mom," said Katie. "She wouldn't understand."

Mrs. Sanchez walked to Katie's bed and sat on the corner by her feet. "What can I do for you, señorita?"

"I have a problem. Two boys asked me to the big school dance, and I said yes to both."

"Oh, my! You do have a problem. You are in trouble."

"Yes, I am," sighed Katie. "I'm in deep, deep trouble, and I can't see how to get out of it. No matter what I do, I will hurt someone's feelings, and I don't want to make either of them feel bad. I wish there were two of me and then I could go to the dance with each of them. But as you can see, there is only one of me, so splitting me in two isn't an option. What should I do?"

"You need to tell the truth. You need to pick the boy you like the best and then tell the other one you can't go with him," said Mrs. Sanchez.

Katie propped herself up in bed, even though her head felt like it would explode, and pulled the covers up over her bent knees. "I know that's what I should do, but I don't dare. I like both, but I like one as a brother and the other as a boyfriend. The problem is that the one I like as a brother has been so nice to me, and I don't want to hurt him."

"You do have a big problem."

"Yes, I do, and I need your advice on how to solve it."

"I'm afraid I don't know what to tell you other than to tell the truth. The truth is always the best answer in all situations. It takes courage to tell the truth. It sometimes makes you uncomfortable, but people prefer to hear the truth and not be lied to. When you lie, you get deeper and deeper into trouble. Lying never solves anything."

"I thought that's what you would say," said Katie with a frown. "Deep in my heart, I know you're right, but I wish there were an easier way out that wouldn't hurt anyone. I don't know what to say."

"When the time comes, you will find the right words. You're a smart girl who'll know what to do."

Katie sighed and slid back down into her bed. "I wish I had as much confidence in me as you do, Mrs. Sanchez."

"Trust me," said Mrs. Sanchez. She stood and walked to the door.

"Thank you for listening. I don't feel any better, but I know you're right. I will tell him I can't attend the dance when Peter comes over today to listen to music."

"That's the right decision." Mrs. Sanchez smiled. "Peter is a good boy, and he will understand. Honesty is the best policy."

Katie stayed in bed the rest of the morning and cuddled with Tex. She tried, once again, to find the right words to tell Peter, but her mind was blank. She didn't know why she couldn't think of something clever to say. *It's the headache that's keeping me from thinking of what to say*, she thought.

After lunch, Katie showered, dressed, and waited for Peter to arrive. Mikey entered her room at two o'clock and announced, "Peter's here."

"Ask him to sit down and let him know I'll be right there," said Katie. She knew it was the right time to tell him. She couldn't mislead him any longer. She took a deep breath and walked into the living room. She felt weak in the knees but knew her decision to tell him the truth was the best course of action.

"Hey, Katie. How are you feeling today?" asked Peter as he stood to greet her.

"A little better," she lied. She realized telling another lie wasn't the best way to start the conversation, so she added, "I do feel tired, and my head hurts."

"That's too bad. I downloaded some new music for us to listen to, but I guess you're not feeling well enough to hear it. It's by the new band you said you wanted to hear. It is their new album. I downloaded it last night. I listened to it before bed. It's good, and I think you'll like it."

"Thank you, Peter. You're so thoughtful." She felt the blood rush to her face, and her cheeks turned red. *Why does he keep making my decision so hard?*

"I also played the music for Sarah and Ryan last night. They came over to the house to see Tennison. They loved the album too. It is quite popular."

Peter's words hit Katie like a slap to her face. They confused her. "What did you just say?" She flopped down on the couch like a bag of dirty laundry. She felt the blood drain from her face, and she thought she was going to faint. *Why was Ryan with Sarah again?*

"I said that Sarah and Ryan came to the house last night.

"Are you sure?" said Katie in disbelief.

"I'm positive. I know who comes to the house. Are you feeling okay?"

"This doesn't make sense." She sighed. "It just doesn't make sense."

"What doesn't make sense? They are Tennison's friends. They come by the house a lot."

"It doesn't make sense that Ryan and Sarah are together so much," she moaned as her head throbbed.

"Why not? He's taking her to the dance in two weeks. I'm sure we'll see them there."

"Peter, there is something I need to tell you." But before she could continue, Tex ran into the room and jumped into Katie's lap. She put her paws on Katie's chest and licked her chin. It made Katie smile.

"Tex sure likes you," said Peter.

"Yes, she does. And I like her." She pushed Tex's paws off her chest and placed them in her lap.

"I like it when you smile," said Peter. "Now what did you want to tell me?"

Katie suddenly felt her courage slip away. She had to tell him now, or she knew she never would. She stared into Tex's furry face so she didn't have to look at Peter. "Peter, I can't go to the dance with you," she blurted out.

❧

CHAPTER 13

Peter stared at her for a few minutes and then smiled. He tilted his head slightly to one side and shrugged his shoulders. "That's okay," he said. "I understand. I always knew you liked Ryan best. It was dreaming on my part to think you'd go to the dance with me. I look foolish right now, don't I? I should have known a pretty girl like you wouldn't go to the dance with a guy like me."

Katie couldn't think of anything to say. She kept her head down and stared at Tex.

"Can we still be friends?" asked Peter. "I would still like to be your friend."

"Sure," she stammered.

"Good. I'd like that very much."

"So would I," she said.

"I guess I should go now," said Peter. "I will come by tomorrow to check on you."

"I'd like that."

Peter stood and left. Katie remained on the couch, petting Tex. Her thoughts bounced inside her head like the little steel ball in a pinball machine. She felt more confused than she had been before her conversation with Peter. And her stomach felt like it was tied up into one gigantic knot. *Why do I feel so funny now that I've told him the truth?*

She set Tex down on the floor and walked to the window. She looked out at Lake Michigan as she tried to collect her thoughts and get her emotions under control. She looked out at the mud-colored water and watched the white sails of the boats blow gently in the wind. While she was deep in thought, the doorbell rang.

"I'll get it," called Mrs. Sanchez. Katie heard the door open.

"Hello, Katie, how are you feeling?"

Katie turned away from the window and saw Tennison standing in the doorway to the living room. "Hey, Tennison," she said weakly.

"I understand you told my brother that you couldn't go to the dance with him. Is that right?"

"Yes, it's true." Katie felt embarrassed.

"Why?"

"I don't know why," Katie lied. The room had an eerie silence as if they were standing in the middle of the huge Chicago City Library. "That's not true," she continued. "The truth is, I told Ryan I would go to the dance with him." Katie watched as Tennison's face turned a bright red. She was mad, and she couldn't disguise her feelings.

"Did you tell Ryan you'd go to the dance with him before or after you told Peter you'd go with him?"

Katie was too embarrassed to answer. She had never done anything like this before. She had always done the right thing. She never tried to hurt another person's feelings. Finally, she got the courage to answer Tennison. "I told Ryan I would go to the dance after I told Peter I would go with him. Ryan asked me to the dance when we were at Navy Pier."

"You know what you did to my brother is wrong, right?"

"I know," replied Katie. She looked at the floor. She was too humiliated to look at Tennison.

"I think Ryan is using you, Katie," said Tennison. "He is using you to make Sarah jealous. I don't think you mean anything to him except as a tool to get back at Sarah. But my brother really likes you. He bought you a dog, and he's come to see you daily while you've been sick. Doesn't that mean anything to you? If you don't watch out, there is a good chance no one will take you to the dance."

Before Katie could answer, Mrs. Sanchez walked into the room. "Do you girls want a Coke or a Sprite to drink?"

"I'm fine," said Katie.

"And I'm leaving," Tennison said with a scowl.

"You're leaving so soon, Ms. Tennison?" asked Mrs. Sanchez. "You just got here."

"Yes, I am. I don't like it here very much, and I'm not sure I like you either, Katie." Tennison turned and walked toward the door.

When Tennison had gone, Mrs. Sanchez looked at Katie. "What was that all about?"

"She wanted to know why I told her brother I wasn't going to the school dance with him."

"Oh, so you finally told him the truth?"

"Yes, I told him the truth, but it doesn't make me feel better. I feel worse. My dad used to tell me that I'd feel better when I told the truth, but he was wrong. I feel miserable. I didn't want to hurt Peter's feelings on purpose, it's that I like Ryan better," said Katie.

"There, there," said Mrs. Sanchez. She took Katie in her arms and squeezed her tightly to her breast. She could feel Katie's muscles convulse with each sob. "I know it hurts, but these are the lessons you must learn as you grow up, Katie. Life isn't easy, and you must face each important decision you make and not run away from them. You've learned a valuable lesson today."

"I don't like learning these lessons," said Katie.

"No one does, but they will make you wiser and smarter as you grow older."

"What am I going to do? I won't have any friends now that Tennison and Peter are mad at me."

The front door opened, and Katie's mom walked in. She was carrying a large sack of groceries. Mrs. Sanchez let go of Katie and ran to take the package out of Dr. Sparrow's arms.

"Katie, what's wrong?" asked Mom.

"Ms. Katie has had a very tough day," answered Mrs. Sanchez. She took the groceries and entered the kitchen, leaving Katie alone with her mother.

"Don't you feel well?"

Katie used the sleeve of her shirt to wipe her tear-stained cheeks. Her eyes were puffy and swollen. "I'm okay."

"You don't look particularly good to me. What happened?"

"I told Peter I couldn't go to the dance with him."

"You did what? I thought you wanted to go to the dance. It's all you've talked about for weeks. What made you change your mind?"

"I didn't change my mind about the dance. I changed my mind about who would take me to the dance. Two boys asked me to the dance, and I had to tell one of them I couldn't go."

Mom sat on the couch. She patted the cushion next to her with her hand and invited Katie to join her. Katie plopped down next to her mom.

"Did you tell both boys you'd go to the dance with them?" asked Mom.

"Yes," said Katie. "Peter asked me first, and I told him I would go with him, but a few days later, Ryan asked me, and I told him yes too."

"Katie, you know what you did was wrong?"

"Yes." Once again, Katie burst into tears. "I did know it was wrong, but I like Ryan more than Peter."

"That doesn't matter. You shouldn't treat people that way. Everyone has feelings, and no one likes to be misled. You should have told Peter as soon as Ryan asked you."

Katie choked back her tears. "I know. But Peter didn't seem upset when I finally told him. It was Tennison who made the big fuss about it."

"Tennison was looking out for her brother, just like you would do for Mikey."

"I guess so."

"I don't know what to tell you. You've dug yourself into this hole. Now, you're going to have to dig yourself out. I suggest you start by calling Tennison and explaining the situation to her. Then you need to call Peter and apologize to him."

"I know you're right, but I'm too embarrassed to call them."

"It's going to be harder the longer you wait," said Mom. She stood and walked toward the kitchen. "I suggest you call them right now."

Katie remained on the couch and played with a button on her shirt. *Why was life so complicated? Why do things have to be so hard?*

She forced herself off the couch and went to her bedroom. She picked up her cell phone and dialed Peter's number.

As she waited for him to answer, Tex jumped on the bed and nuzzled her pink nose into Katie's lap. "At least you still like me," she mumbled. The phone rang five times, and then the answering service picked up. Hurriedly, Katie hung up. She was glad he had not answered. "I will call Tennison tomorrow," she said to Tex. "That will give her time to cool down."

The door to her room banged open, and Mikey walked in with one of his friends.

"Get out of my room," she screamed.

"Make me," he teased.

"I don't make trash. I throw it out. Now get out of my room."

"I can be here if I want," he taunted.

"Not if you want to live. Now scram."

"How come you've been crying? Do you have 'love' problems?" asked Mikey with a mischievous grin.

"It's none of your business."

"I know why. I was down in the lobby and heard your friend Tennison tell your other friend, Sarah, all about how you told Peter you couldn't go to the school dance with him. She also told Sarah that Ryan had asked you to go to the dance too and that you planned on going with him."

"What?" screamed Katie.

"Yeah, Tennison told Sarah about you, Peter, and Ryan. Sarah didn't look so happy about the news."

"Oh no. I thought my life couldn't get any worse, but now it has. I feel like a big, black cloud dumped all its rain over my head. I'm not going to be able to show my face in the building or at school ever again."

"I thought you'd like to hear the news," grinned Mikey. It was obvious he was enjoying every second of Katie's agony. "I've got to run. Cameron and I are going to play Xbox in my room."

Mikey and Cameron laughed as they left the room and slammed the door shut. Katie didn't know whether to laugh or cry. She felt numb. *This can't be happening to me. It just can't be happening. I'll crawl up into a ball and die.*

Katie lay back on her bed, covered her head with her pillow, and screamed.

She didn't know how long she'd been asleep when there was a knock on the door. She opened her eyes. She saw her mother peek around the edge of the door. "Katie, dear, there's a boy here to see you. It's Ryan. He's in the living room."

Katie sprang out of bed. Her heart raced. Ryan was finally here to see her and make everything better. She knew he would. He was her knight in shining armor. "Tell him I'll be right there."

She ran into the bathroom, washed her face, and brushed her hair. She felt happy and alive again. She felt happier than she had in days. She was as happy as the day Peter had brought Tex as a gift. She knew everything was going to be all right again. She didn't care if anyone else liked her as long as Ryan did.

She glanced in the mirror, smiled, and entered the living room.

Ryan sat on the edge of the couch and played with his shirt sleeve. He looked nervous. As Katie entered the room, he sprang to his feet and ran his fingers through his unruly hair.

"Don't stand," said Katie. Ryan sat back on the couch. Katie sat down on one of the side chairs across from the couch. She pulled her feet up under her and squatted. "It's so nice to see you." She had to hold herself back from running over to the couch and wrapping her arms around his neck.

"It's…it's…it's nice to see you too," he stammered.

"I hoped you'd see me soon. I've missed you."

"How are you feeling?"

"Much better now that you're here."

"I'm sorry I didn't see you sooner. I've been busy," said Ryan as he stared at his hands.

"That's okay. I understand. Peter said he's seen you and Sarah often on Michigan Avenue and at his house."

"Yeah, a little bit," said Ryan. There was a long pause. "I understand you told Peter about us going to the dance together."

"Yes, I'm sorry I didn't tell him earlier, but I didn't know how. You know how hard it can be, don't you? Have you told Sarah?"

"That's why I'm here," said Ryan and then coughed. He reached up and wiped a small bead of sweat off his forehead. His face suddenly turned a ghastly pale green color, as if he were going to get sick and throw up.

"Are you okay?" asked Katie. "You don't look so good."

"I'm fine." He coughed again. "Katie, there's something I need to tell you."

"You can tell me anything. What is it?"

"I can't go to the dance with you. I'm taking Sarah."

"What?" she asked in disbelief. "I'm afraid I didn't hear you. I thought you said you were taking Sarah to the dance instead of me. That can't be."

"You heard right. I'm taking Sarah. I was always taking Sarah. I didn't think you would tell me yes when I asked. I knew you had said yes to Peter, and I didn't think you would say yes to me in a million years. I was having some fun—playing a little joke—trying to make Sarah jealous. I didn't think this situation would get so far out of hand. You know how these things go."

"No, I don't know," said Katie as she fought back tears. She put her hand to her mouth to muffle the scream she felt swelling up inside her. She refused to cry. She wasn't going to let Ryan see her pain. She wouldn't let him enjoy his little joke at her expense. "I think you should leave now."

"But—"

"I said you should leave now."

"But I still want to be your friend, Katie. I like you as a friend."

"Friends, don't treat other friends like this."

"Why not? You did the same thing to Peter, and you call him a friend."

Katie couldn't stop herself. She started to cry.

⤝

CHAPTER 14

In the middle of the night, Katie's mom had to call Dr. Williams to come and check on Katie. Her fever had returned, and she had broken out in hives.

Katie's mother paced back and forth in front of the bed while Dr. Williams checked Katie's pulse and blood pressure and listened to her heart through his stethoscope.

"Is she going to be all right?" asked her mother with a worried look.

"Yes, she's fine. She is exhausted. She needs rest. I suggest she stay in bed for several days, get lots of sleep, and drink plenty of fluids. I would also limit the number of people allowed to visit her until she's completely better," said Dr. Williams.

"I don't think you need to worry about anyone visiting me," said Katie. "Everyone here in Chicago hates me. I don't have any friends."

"That can't be true," said Dr. Williams with a surprised look on his oval-shaped face. He took the stethoscope off his neck and placed it into his leather carrying case. "Everyone has a friend."

"I don't."

"That's the fever talking," said Dr. Williams as he turned to talk to Katie's mother.

"She's had a very tough day," said Mom.

"Make sure she gets plenty of rest. Give her one of these pills every four hours. They will help her sleep." Dr. Williams took a small vile of little white pills out of his bag and handed them to Katie's mom. "She should feel better in a day or two. My goal is to have her back on her feet before school starts. She doesn't want to miss the first day of school."

Dr. Williams handed Katie one of the white pills and a glass of water. She tilted her head back and gulped down the pill.

"Thank you for coming to our house tonight," said Mom.

"That's okay," replied Dr. Williams. "Consider it a professional courtesy. One of these days, I will need some dentistry done on my teeth, and it will be your turn to help me."

Mom smiled at Dr. Williams, thanked him again, and then led him to the door. He turned, winked at Katie, and exited the room.

Even with the help of the sleeping pill, Katie couldn't sleep. She tossed and turned in her bed as she replayed her conversation with Ryan repeatedly in her head. She felt sorry for herself, and it hurt that he had treated her so badly. Her pain soon turned to anger. *How could he treat me this way? Somehow, I'll get even with him. I will have my revenge. I want him to feel as bad as he has made me feel.*

"What goes around comes around," she muttered. But then she realized that if she felt this way about Ryan, then Peter must feel the same way about her. *Oh no*, she thought, *Peter is probably planning some sort of trick on me right now to get even. He's lying in bed plotting a mean joke to play on me.*

The thoughts of Peter seeking revenge soon made her anger toward Ryan disappear. For the first time, she realized that she was just as much to blame for her present predicament as Ryan. She realized she was the one who had said yes to different boys about going to the dance. She had been blinded by Ryan's good looks and charm, which made her break her promise to Peter. She recognized that this stupid, stinking mess was her fault.

"I have to correct my mistake," she said out loud. "There is no one else that can repair this situation. Tomorrow, I'll call Peter, apologize, and tell him I can go to the dance with him." The decision to say she was sorry to Peter made her feel better and calmed her. She stopped tossing and turning and drifted off to sleep.

The next morning, she woke with a terrible headache and still felt feverish. She ached all over, but the only thing on her mind was to call Peter and apologize. She looked at the clock on her nightstand. With her head pounding, she reached for her phone, but before she could punch in the numbers, her mother walked into the room.

"What do you think you're doing?" scolded Mom. "Dr. Williams specifically said you're to rest in bed all day, and you're not supposed to have visitors. That means no phone calls either." Her mother quickly walked to the side of Katie's bed and took her phone. "I'll take this with me. I want you to get better. That means following Dr. Williams's orders. Do you understand?"

"But I must make a phone call. It's especially important," pleaded Katie.

"Nothing is more important than your health."

"This phone call is. If I don't make this call, my life as I know it is ruined forever."

"Don't be so melodramatic, Katie. You're not the only person in the world experiencing a crisis. Why don't you think of others for a change? Just look at me. I'm trying to establish my dentistry practice, raise a family, and care for a sick daughter. That's a lot of pressure for a single mom. So please cooperate and take care of yourself so it's one less thing I need to worry about."

Katie sat up in her bed and looked at her mother. "That's so unfair of you to say. I've taken care of myself since Daddy passed away. For the past nine months, I've been the mom of this family. I've been the one who has babysat and played with Mikey, packed boxes for the move to Chicago, unpacked boxes when we got here, helped Mrs. Sanchez set up the house, and cooked the meals. That sounds like 'mom work' to me. You're never around. When you are, you're either sleeping or getting ready to leave again. I want my old mom back." She hit the top of the pillow she had placed in her lap with her fist. The sudden movement made Tex jump off the bed and bark.

"That's enough out of you, Katie. Not only are you confined to your room until you're well, but I'm taking your phone away for a month. You're even forbidden to call Camden. It's a good thing you don't have a date for the dance because I would make you cancel that too. I've heard enough from your smart mouth. I want you to know I'm trying as hard as I can to hold this family together and make things work for us, and no one helps me by doing what I ask."

Katie sighed and slumped back into her bed. She put the pillow over her head and cried. Between her sobs, she heard the door slam as her mother left the room. It was no use worrying now. Her life was officially ruined. She had no friends, her mother hated her, and she was sick again. Life couldn't get any worse.

She stayed in bed for the next two days, and as her mother had promised, she didn't return her phone. She filled her days playing with Tex, working on Sudoku puzzles, reading books, and talking to Mrs. Sanchez. As each day passed, she felt sadder and sadder because no one came to visit, not even Mikey. She had never felt so isolated and alone in her life. It was like living on a different planet.

On Saturday morning, she woke up early. Her head didn't hurt, and she felt normal again. She slipped out of bed and walked to the kitchen to get a drink of milk. She got a cookie from the cookie jar, walked to the counter, and ate it as she sipped the ice-cold milk. It tasted great.

On the counter was an envelope. It was addressed to her. She picked it up and looked at it. It didn't have a stamp, and there was no postage mark in the right-hand corner. *This letter must have been hand-delivered*, she thought. She took a butter knife from the drawer, placed the edge under the flap, and sliced it open. She reached inside the envelope and took out the card. On the front, it said "Get well soon" with a cartoon picture of a dog in a hospital bed with an ice pack on its forehead and a thermometer sticking out of its mouth. The picture made her smile.

She opened the card and read it. It said, "Katie, I'm sorry you're not feeling well again. I want you to know I stopped by yesterday to talk to you, but Mrs. Sanchez wouldn't let me in. So I'm sending you this card to let you know I'm thinking about you. Take care, Peter."

She closed the card and held it to her chest. *Peter is thinking about me*, she thought. *I'm saved.* She felt happy.

She had a plan. She would wait until her mother left for work, and then she would sneak to the kitchen, use the phone, and call Peter. She would tell him she could go to the dance with him. Things were starting to turn around. Things were looking brighter, and a smile crept across her pale face for the first time in days. *This is going to be a good day*, she thought.

She went back to her room and took a hot shower. It was the first time she'd showered and shampooed her hair in several days. It made her feel alive and gave her new energy. Tex stood in the doorway to the bathroom and watched as she blew her hair dry and brushed it until it shone.

She was dressed in a pair of comfortable jeans and a sleeveless yellow blouse. She slid a pair of white cotton socks on her feet and put on her slippers. She sat on her bed and waited for her mother to leave. It seemed like forever before she heard the front door slam shut.

She opened the bedroom door a crack and peeked down the hall. She heard Mrs. Sanchez in Mikey's room attempting to get him dressed. She opened her door and snuck down the hallway. She crept to the kitchen on her tiptoes. She had to make the phone call quickly before Mrs. Sanchez was through dressing Mikey.

She picked up the receiver, put it to her ear, and hastily tapped in Peter's phone number. As the phone rang, her heart beat faster and faster as she waited for him to pick up. *Please hurry and answer*, she thought, *before I lose my nerve.*

He finally picked up the call on the fifth ring. "Hello."

"Peter?" she whispered.

"Yes."

"Peter, this is Katie. Katie Sparrow."

"Why are you whispering?"

"It's a long story, and I don't have much time."

"Okay. I was sorry that Ryan couldn't take you to the dance."

"You heard about that?"

"I don't know anyone that hasn't heard about his cruel joke."

"Oh." She sighed. "That's why I'm calling."

Peter was silent. She hoped he would say something, but there was only silence on the other end. *Why doesn't he make this easy on me and ask me to go to the dance now? He knows that I'm not going with Ryan*, she wondered. She said, "First, thank you for the get-well card. It worked. I feel much better."

"I'm glad to hear it. I was worried about you."

"That's the nicest thing anyone's said to me in a couple of days."

"How's Tex?"

"She's fine," replied Katie. "The second reason I called was to let you know I can go to the dance with you."

Once again, there was silence on the other end. *Why doesn't he say something, she thought? Is he trying to make me beg him to take me to the dance? If that's what he wants, that's what I'll do.*

"Peter, did you hear me? I said I could go to the dance with you."

"I heard you," said Peter after a long pause.

"Well?"

"I'm sorry, Katie, I've decided not to go to the dance this year. And since I'm not attending the dance, I can't take you."

Katie was stunned. She couldn't believe her ears. Her knees wobbled and felt weak like they had turned from bone and muscle to liquid. Her head spun, and she felt like she was going to faint and collapse on the floor. *That's not what he was supposed to say. He was supposed to say yes and was glad and excited to take me to the dance. He's not following my plan.* "I thought you said we were still friends."

"We are," said Peter, "but I don't want to go to the dance."

The last thing Katie remembered was hanging up the receiver. Everything else was a blur for the rest of the day.

CHAPTER 15

The next day, Katie didn't bother to get out of bed. She lay there and thought about how messed up her life was and that there was probably no hope of making it better. The only thing she had to look forward to now was the first day of school and the potential of meeting new friends.

How did things turn out so wrong? she wondered. *Why did I have to like Ryan so much? I should have seen right from the start that he was shallow and self-centered. I should have seen how much he liked Sarah by the amount of time he spent with her. I should have known a good-looking guy like Ryan wouldn't want to spend time with a plain little country girl like me. I should have liked Peter from the start.*

She knew she couldn't turn back time and go back to the beginning, back to when this situation began. She wished she could go back and make everything right. But she was a realist. She knew there was no way to fix it, and she would have to live with the consequences of her decisions.

At noon, Mrs. Sanchez brought a hot bowl of chicken soup and crackers into her room on one of her mother's large serving trays. She helped Katie sit up and propped pillows behind her back to make her comfortable.

Mrs. Sanchez sat on the corner of the bed and watched as Katie sipped the soup. "How does the soup taste, Ms. Katie?"

"It's good, but I don't have much appetite."

"You need to keep up your strength so you can get better. It won't be long before school starts."

"I have no reason to get better," said Katie. "My life has been turned upside down, and there is no way to turn it right side up. I don't even think school will help."

"Why do you say such things?"

"Because I've lost every friend here in Chicago because of my lies. I've lost Ryan, Peter, and Tennison. Sarah never liked me, so losing her friendship doesn't hurt as much as losing the others."

"Shush, Ms. Katie, that kind of talk is nonsense. You will make many friends once you start school. And there will be a lot of boys to choose from for future dances. One thing I know is there are a lot of good boys in the world, and you want to make sure you meet as many as you can as you grow older so you can pick the one that is right for you. That's what I did. I met a lot of boys when I was growing up; some were short, some were tall, some were fat, and some were skinny. Some boys I met were very smart while others were rather dull. There were handsome boys and ugly boys, and even boys with warts and pimples."

"I know." Katie sighed.

"The one thing I learned is that boys come in all shapes and sizes. I learned that it didn't matter what a boy looked like if he treated me well and made me laugh. That's my husband, Jose. He may not be the most handsome man in the world, but he treats me like his queen and makes me laugh."

"You were lucky to find Jose," said Katie. "I'm sure I won't be that lucky. I've never been lucky. All my luck is bad." She put another spoonful of soup in her mouth.

"We make our luck," said Mrs. Sanchez. "Things always work out if you keep a positive mental attitude and think good thoughts. Bad luck follows those who give up or don't try anymore. You're not a quitter, Ms. Katie. I know you'll fight back and be happy."

Katie swallowed some more soup, but it went down her windpipe this time, and she coughed. Mrs. Sanchez leaned over, reached behind Katie, and patted her back. "You must not gulp your food, Ms. Katie."

"Thank you, Mrs. Sanchez. I wish you were my mom."

"I will be like a mother to you."

After she finished her soup, she fell asleep and slept until she heard a knock on the door. She opened her eyes and looked around. It was dark. She looked at the clock on her nightstand; it read eight o'clock. She realized she'd slept all afternoon and into the evening. She looked at the door as it opened. She saw her mother's head peer around the door.

"Katie, are you awake?"

"Yes."

"Can we talk?"

Katie didn't want to talk to her mother. She knew her mother didn't understand her. Her mother didn't know how hurt she was and how raw her emotions were. The situation with Ryan and Peter had put her in a tailspin, and she didn't know how to get out of it. She didn't want to have another argument with her mom. "Mom, can we do it some other time?"

"No, I think it is time for us to have mother and daughter talk."

"Okay," said Katie reluctantly. Katie watched as her mother tip-toed into her room. Her mother didn't bother to turn on the lights but made her way to the bed using the dim light from the hallway. She sat on the bed and put her hand on Katie's cheek.

"How are you feeling tonight?" asked Mom.

"A little better," she lied. Her body felt fine; but her heart was broken, her mind was a mess, and she knew there wasn't any medicine in the world that could cure those two aches and pains.

"I'm glad you're feeling better."

"Did you wake me up just so you could ask me how I felt?"

"No, not exactly," her mother said. "I want to talk about us. I want to talk about what a bad mother I've been the last several months. I want you to know how sorry I am about the way I've treated you since your father passed away."

Katie couldn't believe her ears. *I must be dreaming*, she thought. *This can't be my mother saying these things.* She pinched her leg under the sheet to see if she was awake. "Ouch!" She was wide awake.

"What's wrong?"

"Nothing," said Katie. She had difficulty figuring out who this mystery woman was in front of her. She looked like her mother. It sounded like her mother's voice. She smelled her mother's perfume, but the words coming out of this woman's mouth were alien to her. These words were kind and gentle and not mean and sarcastic.

"I've been very selfish the past few months," the strange person said. "I've only been thinking about me, and I haven't spent enough time thinking of what's best for you and Mikey. I feel ashamed."

Katie listened to this strange woman who looked like her mother. She watched as this stranger sniffed her nose and wiped her eyes with her hands. She realized the person in front of her was crying. She put her hand out and touched the stranger on the knee. It felt like her mother too.

"I've been very selfish and self-centered," the alien creature sobbed. "I don't blame you for hating me because of how I've treated you. I've only thought about what I need and want. I haven't taken the time to find out what you need and want.

"It was hard for me when your father died. He was my best friend. I was mad and hurt that he had left us. I was hurt because I knew I would never see him again and mad because he had left me to raise two kids. I was certain the world was going to come to an end and quit spinning. I've been so caught up in my sorrow and loss that I haven't helped you through your pain and hurt."

"Mom, please stop crying."

"I can't until you forgive me for how I've acted."

Katie sat in the darkness and looked at her mother's silhouette, outlined by the yellow light that trickled into her room from the hallway. Her mother had hurt her deeply the past few months, and she wasn't sure she could forgive her. All the mean things her mother had said and done since her father's death flooded her thoughts, and she lay in silence in the darkness.

"Did you hear me?" asked Mom.

After a few more minutes of awkward silence, Katie whispered, "Yes, Mom, I heard you."

"So can you forgive me?"

"This is awfully sudden," said Katie. "I haven't had time to think."

"But I need to know tonight. I won't be able to sleep until I know you've forgiven me."

Katie loved her mother, at least the mother she had known before her father's death. She wanted her old mother back so badly.

She wondered if her mother could change. "Mom, I don't want you to ask me to forgive you unless you mean it and you can change."

"I can change. I really can," sobbed Mom. "I want to change. I want to be the mother you want me to be. I promise."

Katie threw her arms around her mother's neck and kissed her on the cheek. "I love you, Mom. I forgive you. I will try to be a better daughter too. I've done some stupid things the past few weeks. I will try to be the daughter you want me to be. I promise."

Katie and her mother remained embraced for what seemed like an eternity. Both cried, and their tears mingled and fell in their laps like raindrops.

That night, Katie slept like a log, as if she didn't have a worry or care. It felt like a dark cloud had disappeared above her head, and a heavy weight had been lifted off her shoulders. She felt new and fresh. And she dreamed. She dreamed of Alpine, Camden, her father, and how happy she was to be alive. She dreamed of her mother and the times they had baked cookies together. She dreamed of summers spent swimming with Mikey in their pool. And she dreamed of Tex and how her pink tongue felt when she licked her face. The only thing she didn't dream about was Ryan, Sarah, or Peter. It was as if her mind had been cleared of the drama and clutter of the past several weeks.

The next morning, when she woke, she felt like her old self again. She felt like she could conquer the world and overcome any obstacles. She jumped out of bed, anxious to shower, and start a new day; but as she did, an envelope slipped off her pillow and fell on the floor. She stooped down and picked it up. Her name was printed on the front in her mother's handwriting. She tore open the envelope and pulled out a clean, crisp piece of her mother's writing paper. She unfolded it and read the contents out loud. "Dear Katie. Thank you so much for talking to me last night. I love you very much. Love, Mom. PS: Peter will be here at ten this morning, so please shower and fix your hair."

What does this mean? she wondered. *Why would Peter be coming to my house today? This doesn't make sense.* She folded the writing paper, put it back in the envelope, and set it on her desk.

She hurried into the bathroom and took a long, hot shower. She stayed in the shower until her skin was pink and wrinkled. She dried herself with a large, fluffy white towel and combed her freshly washed hair. She pulled it back into a ponytail. She flossed and brushed her teeth until they sparkled then slipped into her favorite jeans and one of her new shirts.

"Ms. Katie," called Mrs. Sanchez from the living room. "There's a young man here to see you."

Katie took one final look at herself in the mirror, pulled a few strands of wayward hair off her forehead, and stuck them back. She put on her slippers as she left the room and walked down the hallway to the living room.

Peter stood by the bookshelf, examining the titles of the books. He had his back to her. When she entered the room, he turned around and gave her a toothy grin. "Katie, you look beautiful. It's so good to see you looking so well."

"It's good to see you too. Have a seat."

Peter sat on the couch, and Katie sat across from him in one of the side chairs. He looked so handsome. For a few minutes, neither said a word but stared at each other.

"Finally," Peter said. "Your mother called me this morning."

"My mother did what?"

"Your mother called me this morning. She explained many things to me about your relationship with her, how it was her fault for the mix-up on the school dance. She said I shouldn't blame you for what happened but blame her because of the way she had treated you."

"She said all that?"

"Yes, and a lot more. She said you wanted to go to the dance with me and that you would accept if I asked you to go again. Is that true?"

"Are you asking me to the dance? I thought you told me you didn't want to go to the dance now?"

"Your mother made it clear that it was her fault for how you acted and the confusion it caused. So, Katie Sparrow, will you go to the dance with me?"

"Yes, Peter, I would love to go to the dance with you. There is nothing I would like better."

"Even more than Ryan?"

"I've learned that Ryan is a shallow, thoughtless boy and that Sarah deserves him. They are the perfect couple: self-centered, egotistical, and shallow. I don't like those kinds of people. I want to go to the dance with someone caring and not afraid to be themselves. That's why I would be honored to go to the dance with you." Katie smiled warmly at Peter. It was the first time she was sure she was doing the right thing. She loved her new self-confidence.

"Great," said Peter, "I can't wait."

Almost on cue, Tex leaped off the floor and landed in Peter's lap. She put her front paws on his chest and licked his chin. Peter burst out laughing. "Well, it looks like Tex is happy too."

The rest of the morning seemed to float by. She cleaned her room, made her bed, and straightened her closet. She had more energy than she had for a long time.

Katie ate her lunch with Mrs. Sanchez in the kitchen. They had a bowl of soup and a tuna fish sandwich, which they washed down with a large glass of milk. When the front door opened, they had just put their dishes in the sink.

Mrs. Sanchez looked at Katie in surprise. "I wonder who that could be? Mikey's not supposed to be home from Stewart's house until four o'clock."

Katie ran into the living room to see who was there. It was her mother. "Mom, what are you doing home so early?" Her mother had never come home this early before.

Mom looked at Katie warmly and said, "I'm home early because I'm spending the rest of the afternoon on Michigan Avenue with my daughter. The receptionist changed my schedule and moved my patients to a different day. I told them I was spending the day with the most important person in the world. I realized last night we had a lot of catching up to do. We also need a new dress and shoes for the big dance."

The End

ABOUT THE AUTHOR

Steve F. Hallsey is the author of the popular children's book *Matilda McGruder*. He is a former college football coach at the University of Utah and was the president and CEO of several large national real estate companies. He retired from business in 2023 to dedicate his time to his passion for writing, carving, sculpting, and painting. He and his wife split their time between their ranch in Utah and their cabin in the Blue Ridge Mountains of Georgia.

www.ingramcontent.com/pod-product-compliance
Lightning Source LLC
Chambersburg PA
CBHW031430130726
47989CB00003B/1080